KIDNAPPED BY AN OUTLAW

IVY MCADAMS

Kidnapped by an Outlaw — Emerald Falls Book 1
by Ivy McAdams

https://ivymcadams.com

Emerald Falls Series

Kidnapped by an Outlaw

Seduced by a Wrangler

Captivated by a Gunslinger

Emerald Falls Novella

Rescued by a Desperado

CHAPTER 1

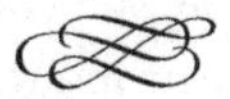

A wave of tan-backed pronghorn swarmed over the green hillside beside the moving train. Sadie Tanner gazed out the glass window at the bobbing black horns and the spry deer-like bodies as they bounded and sprang in unison like a flock of birds on the ground. The excitement of the endless prairie before them, ultimate freedom, had to be the best feeling.

Sadie propped her chin in her hand with a sigh, wishing she could trade the hours-long ride in a stuffy train car to run in the grass with them. Wind in her hair and sunshine on her face.

"I should have picked up that coat I saw in the window," a gruff voice mumbled as it approached. "A fella back there said he heard the winter was gone be a cold one."

An older man with long legs clad in black trousers and a blue button-up shirt sat in the seat next to her. His dark hair streaked with lines of gray was swept back over his crown, held back by a few licks of pomade. She'd never in her life seen Papa so fancied up.

"The coat you have now is fine," she said, shifting away

from the window to address him. "We'll need that extra money for our rations. Especially now."

Jed Tanner was a careful planner. They'd been living on the outskirts of the small town of Emerald Falls for over a decade, surviving off the land and only going into town for extra supplies. He'd been trapping, tanning, and living the merchant life for as long as she could remember. He knew how to be frivolous with their money.

Until he was faced with the bitter truth that the little money they had might not save them.

"The elk could still come in," she murmured as she rested a hand on his arm.

He rubbed his fingers over the shadow of hair on his chin as he nodded. "They could. I've never known them not to come, but things ain't lookin' good."

She gnawed at her inner cheek as she forced a reassuring smile.

"They'll get here."

He nodded slowly as he leaned back in his seat and fished a dark felt hat out of his pocket to drape over his face. He didn't like train rides, but more than that, she knew he didn't want to talk about it.

He'd shocked her the night before by announcing his plan to scout St. Aspen for a job. Never in her life had he held a job in town. The elk herd that usually flooded the valley in the shadow of the Absaroka Mountains that time of year was an entire month late, leaving Papa in a fret that their biggest money-maker for the autumn season wouldn't show.

They wouldn't survive the winter without the money and food the herd brought.

So that morning she'd dressed in one of her mother's soft yellow lace dresses and accompanied Papa beyond their small town to the bigger city of St. Aspen so he could beg for work.

It hadn't gone well.

Sadie stared out the window once more, wishing she hadn't offered to come on the trip at all. It was exhausting, and she felt dirty from traveling. She'd have to wash up that night, as she had a noon tea the next day to look forward to.

Robert Murphy, whose father was one of the most well-known cattle ranchers in all of Wyoming, would accompany her. The thought tugged a smile to her lips.

Some days she felt Papa didn't have his head on quite straight, making them live out in the woods instead of Emerald Falls proper, but he'd made a fine match when he'd picked Robert Murphy for her. The man was handsome, well-groomed, and quite the gentleman. She'd been courting him for nearly a month, and she couldn't wait to become a rancher's wife and return to life in Emerald Falls, to be reunited with the other women she'd went to school with as a child.

She pressed a finger to the cool glass as a pair of coyotes darted in and out of the underbrush in the wake of the pronghorn herd. Soon she'd be free and happy, just like the animals on the hills.

"I'm going to get some air, maybe a bite," Papa said suddenly as he sat up. "You need anything?"

"I'm fine, Papa. Thank you."

His small frame moved down the aisle between the rows of seats and disappeared out the door at the front of the car. A burst of chilly air swept in and ruffled the hem of Sadie's dress. She crossed her ankles with a shiver.

With Papa gone, the soft hum of voices rolled up and down the car. Most of the passengers were men in suits. A few wives dotted the seats toward the back, and they leaned in to talk and titter to one another. Across the aisle and a few seats back, two young ladies, a couple years her junior by the looks of them, paged through a catalog and whispered.

Sadie'd just turned to glance out the window again when a door slammed. The scream from the back of the car made Sadie jump. She twisted in her seat as another woman at the rear of the unit shrieked and leapt up.

Two men dressed in black stood at the end of the aisle. One pressed a hand on the hysterical woman's shoulder and shoved her back into her seat.

The men were the same height and wore identical black handkerchiefs over their faces. The eyes over the masks were hard and bore into each of the car's occupants. When one pair found her, Sadie's breath stopped.

The man pulled a revolver from the gun belt slung around his hips and pointed it to the nearest man, the husband of the woman he'd pushed. The gentleman had gotten to his feet with a stern look etched into his brow as if he meant to reprimand the stranger, but once the gun barrel was pointed at his forehead, the fellow took his seat again.

"Nobody move," the man in black spoke. "I'm here for your valuables. Hand them over and no one has to get hurt."

Sadie clutched her hands against her chest and lowered into her seat.

Train robbers!

A woman screamed again, and a man with a wide white mustache just a few seats back from Sadie growled obscenities.

The dark eyes of the armed man shot toward them and narrowed.

"Take a seat," the thief roared.

When the passenger didn't budge, the man in black took two long strides toward him and swung the revolver into his face. The handlebars on man's face quivered as the gun struck him, and he sank into his seat.

"Now," the bandit barked. "Hand over your goods, and we won't have to search you."

He turned fierce eyes on the mustached man, and the passenger yanked a pocket watch from his vest. He handed it over without another word.

"Thank you, kind sir," the man in black growled with an amused twinkle in his eye. "You next." He pointed to the next seat and moved on.

The second thief was making his way up her side of the aisle, holding an open saddle bag out for passengers to drop items in. He brandished no gun but grunted a deep growl when anyone hesitated.

“Drop it in,” he huffed at a cowboy she recognized from Emerald Falls.

“Who do you think you are, just swiping our things like this?” The passenger said, shoving his hands into his pockets defiantly. “The sheriff will be on your tail in no time.”

The man in black wasn’t as tall as the cowboy, but he outweighed him. He had wide shoulders and a solid build. Like he could take that cowboy out without a weapon at all.

“I’m not afraid of no sheriff,” the thief hissed.

“You should be.” The cowboy glowered, pushing his hands deeper into his pockets.

The outlaw lowered the saddlebag, caught the passenger around the throat with his other hand, and pressed him against the car wall. A woman next to them shrieked and shied away. The cowboy fell back with wide eyes, hands leaping from his pockets to the vice on his neck.

“You think a sheriff is gon’ save you right now, boy?” the man in black growled.

Despite the jut of his chin, the cowboy’s nostrils flared, and he blinked wide eyes. The fingers on his throat flexed, and he shook his head with a bleat of apology.

“No, no, sir. Ain’t no one out to help me here.”

“Didn’t think so.”

“Clay!” the thief with the gun grunted from the center of

the aisle. He'd gone through half the car already. "Quit making friends and let's get out of here."

His partner narrowed his eyes and released the cowboy. Then he shoved the edge of the saddlebag into the man's chest.

"Don't make me come get it."

The passenger fumbled into his pocket and produced a money clip. Clay nodded his approval as he took the cash and tossed it into his satchel. Then he moved on.

The thieves advanced to the front, seat by seat.

Sadie's chest felt tight. She didn't have anything of value on her. Would they believe that? She wore a simple dress, leather boots, and a few barrettes in her hair. It'd only been a day trip, so the small bag she brought only held a catalog she'd picked up and a book.

The armed man struck a short man across the temple with his revolver, and Sadie jumped. A commotion followed, drowned out by the thief's roar.

"Now, I said!"

Sadie glanced toward the front door of the car where Papa had disappeared. She was only two seats away from it. She might be able to make it out of the car before the thieves caught her. Papa would protect her.

She silently swung her boots down to the maroon carpeted floor. The idiots were so greedy that they might not even notice her leave.

As a woman in the back began to cry, Sadie got to her feet and braced a hand on Papa's seat. Neither man looked in her direction. She eased a boot into the center aisle.

One of the robbers grunted, and she froze. But they weren't looking in her direction.

The armed man nudged his companion and nodded toward the rear of the car.

"Someone's heading this way. Let's get a move on."

A storage car followed them, and Sadie could see it bumping along in the back windows. A train worker was walking through the car. He stopped to check a box here and there, in no rush. Yet.

"Move up a car," Clay's deep voice rumbled.

The two men took a few long strides down the center aisle. Sadie ducked back into her seat.

"Cough it up," the armed man grumbled as he stopped. His voice wasn't as deep, but it was raspy. Like he was fighting a whisper.

The man he'd stopped at handed over a few bills.

Clay stopped once more for a pearl necklace before stepping up alongside Sadie. His face was half covered by his mask, and the low brim of his black hat did well to hide the rest of it, but his eyes caught hers before he spoke a word.

A soft blue popped from the darkness. Like the depths of the lake in wintertime. Vivid and sharp. A hidden cavern you might get lost in if you swam too far.

She stared as her fingers trembled on the back of the chair.

"Valuables?" he murmured. His voice was so low she thought for a moment she'd only imagined he'd said it.

Her head shook just a fraction. "I have none," she whispered.

Eyes still locked on her, he nodded. Then he was gone.

The men rushed to the front of the car and disappeared through the door into the cool air.

A man shouted in the back of the car after the thieves were gone. Women called out and whimpered, hugging onto one another. Sadie collapsed into her seat, pressing a hand to her chest as she gulped down a breath of relief. She'd made it out of the encounter without an issue.

Except she'd never seen eyes so captivating. So raw and fierce. Eyes that had probably seen people die and live to the fullest all in one day. There was nothing mundane and wanting in those eyes. They were alive.

And the way they'd held hers so tightly. The memory stole her breath away.

Sadie leaned out into the aisle once again, hoping to catch one more glance at Clay's solid blue stare.

What she found instead made her gasp and rush for the door.

CHAPTER 2

The weapon-brandishing thief shoved his free hand into the collar of Papa's shirt and lifted him off the ground. Sadie's throat clenched at the sight of the silver revolver pressed up alongside her father's cheek.

She clung to the inside of the car door, watching as the robbers crowded Papa. The blood in her veins turned to ice, and her fingers trembled.

Give them whatever they want!

They couldn't take him from her. He was all she had in the world.

She shoved the door open, and the cool evening air whipped her in the face. Green fields and trees rushed by in a blur, and she drew in close to the car wall with a gasp. There would be no way to help Papa if she fell between the blasted train carts.

Sadie reached out for the handrail and crept toward the edge of the ramp. The buzz in the bar and step rattled up through her body. She could easily lose her footing and fall to her death. Her dress could get hung on a loose screw and jerk her off course.

But Papa needed her.

She could hear the muffled voices of the men shouting. The armed man shook Papa again.

Resolve hardened within her. She pushed forward another step and leaned from one car to the next. She clung to the railing on the second car, hauling herself over to its ledge with a hiss of nerves. Then she rushed to the car door and shoved her way inside.

"Tom, let him down," Clay said as he pushed his accomplice in the shoulder. "He can't answer you if you don't—"

All three men turned to her as she sprinted in.

Those dark blue eyes were locked on hers instantly, and she felt a moment of weakness come over her. She'd nearly forgotten why she came busting in. She had been looking for those eyes, after all.

But then she'd spotted Papa.

She frowned at the men and pointed a finger.

"You let him go."

Papa's eyes were wide, and he stuttered. "Sadie, no. Get out."

Tom turned a sharp frown on her and spun Papa out of the way. "So who is Miss Sadie?"

His dark eyes were fierce, and she stumbled back a step.

"No one!" Papa burst, wrestling against Clay's arm pressed across his chest.

Tom pushed them farther back, unfazed by the outburst. His eyes narrowed, and he nodded his chin in Sadie's direction.

"What's your family name, girl?"

She hesitated, observing each man in turn. Clay had fallen silent, but his eyes were vigilant. Her father's were wide and twitched as he shook his head a fraction. But Tom's were on fire, scorching the edges of her confidence. His revolver was much too close to Papa's head. Dread knotted in her stomach like a stone.

"Sadie Tanner."

Papa closed his eyes, and an evil grin spread over Tom's face. He shook her father again. "I thought you said you were alone, old man? Seems to me you got a pretty little lady here with you."

Sadie bit her lip and backed up another step until the door handle dug into her back. She'd walked right into a trap.

"We got all we need then," Tom said. "Get her. Let's get out of here."

He pressed the gun barrel into Papa's temple and shoved him down the aisle toward the front of the car. Sadie rushed to follow, but Clay grabbed her around the waist.

His arms were hard and strong, lifting her right off her feet and onto his hip. She shrieked and flailed against his body.

"Put me down!"

"Let her go," Papa pleaded as they were herded to the front of the car.

"Hush your mouth," Tom spat.

The car was much less populated than the one they'd been sitting in. The few passengers aboard drew back in horror as the group passed them. Sadie pushed against Clay and kicked her legs out at the seats they passed, hoping to catch one well enough to pull herself back.

"Help!" she screamed at a pair of men that watched her go by.

One looked as white as a sheep while the other glowered.

"Let those people go," the angry one shouted. "Less we need to take this matter into our own hands."

Tom wheeled his gun around on the passenger and shot him square in the chest. Sadie screamed, and the car buzzed with shocked and terrified voices as the man dropped to the floor.

"Move," Tom snarled and shoved Papa the last few feet to the front of the car.

He slung it open and stepped outside. Clay followed, lowering Sadie to her feet and taking a firm grip on her arm.

Her insides had run cold. They'd shot a man. A stranger. Were she and her father going to be next? Her head screamed to follow all directions to keep herself safe, but her instincts had her determined to fight her way out.

She wrenched against Clay's grip, but he pushed her forward like she was a simple rag doll.

Papa and the filthy murderer stood at the edge of the car platform. Tom fit a pair of fingers to his lips and blew a harsh whistle. Clay followed suit, and Sadie plugged her ears with a gasp.

"What in the blazes are you two doing?" she spat. "Let us go."

"We have better things in mind for you, Miss Tanner," Tom shouted over the thunder of the tracks below. "You're going to make us a lot of money."

She skewed her face at him angrily. They barely had enough funds to make it through the winter. That is if they didn't actually starve. They had nothing of value the men could take.

She lifted a hand to question his idiotic statement when the sound of hoofbeats lifted above the shrill train wheels on the track. She frowned, leaning nearer to Papa to see over the edge of the platform.

The head of a black galloping horse appeared not ten feet from the edge of the track.

Sadie blinked in surprise.

"What the—"

Before her shock could settle, a buckskin with a flashy cream coat came along behind it.

"Your chariot awaits," Tom cackled over his shoulder at her.

She wrinkled her nose in distaste at the sharpness of his laugh. The way his eyes pierced through her and dismissed her as if she were a mere trinket he'd picked up from the street.

"You don't mean to…" Papa coughed and inched away from his captor.

Tom pushed Papa up to the edge of the platform as the horse drew closer.

"Don't be yellow, old man. I know you've ridden a horse before."

Sadie gasped, realizing their intent.

"Are you crazy?" she gasped, pulling against Clay's grasp. "We can't get to that horse. We're going too fast."

"Shut her up," Tom snarled, waving his gun again.

Clay's grip on her arm tightened, and she pressed her lips together with a soft prayer.

"Now, are you ready, old man?" Tom asked. "I'm going to count, and we're going to jump."

"Down there?" Papa sputtered.

"Right onto the back of ol' Hound Dog. He's done this dozens of times. He'll be fine."

"B-but I can't make that jump."

"You can, and you will. When I get to three. Else we'll throw Miss Tanner here off the other side, you hear?"

Papa's eyes met hers, big and full of concern. Then he gave a stuttering nod. "Yes."

Tom holstered his gun, took a firm grip on Papa's upper arm, and lined them up as he counted. On three, both men leapt off the side and landed hard on the horse's back. Tom straddled the saddle while Papa hit the cantel with his stomach, snatching for a hold to keep himself upright.

Sadie's hands flew to her mouth with a gasp, but Tom reached back to help haul Papa up onto the edge of his saddle. Then they pulled away from the train and slowed.

"Oh, my lands," she breathed, fanning at her face with her hand. "That was insanity."

A soft grunt of a chuckle rattled in Clay's chest. "We're next."

Sadie turned on him with a nervous hiss. "Are you kidding? We can't—"

"We sure can."

His blue eyes sparkled at her, and for a moment, she felt compelled to believe him. But no—it was outrageous. Jumping off a moving train? She didn't have a death wish.

His fingers closed around her bicep, and she jerked her arm. But his hand was like a vice on her, and she bit back a cry as his fingers pinched into her skin.

"We don't have much time." His voice had lowered. A stern whisper. She felt herself leaning in to hear him better. "I'm going to jump. You are going to follow me."

"No, I can't," she whimpered, tugging away.

He held her still. "You will. If you don't jump after me, we'll take your pappy on down to the river, and you'll never see him again."

A tremble tickled up through her feet and legs, and she nodded. She couldn't let these hoodlums have her father. He was the only family she had left in the world. Or at least the only one that cared about her.

"You ready?" Clay asked, moving her closer to the edge.

The ground rushed by beneath them at a blurring speed. Her stomach turned. The wheels on the track screamed, and the horse beside them snorted out heavy breaths. It was growing weary.

Sadie swallowed her nerves.

A commotion in the car turned their heads. Through the window, most of the passengers were on their feet, pointing. A train car worker held a revolver out in front of him as he stalked down the aisle.

Sadie's breath caught in her throat. She could be saved! But what of Papa? She peered out over the edge to look for him, but he and Tom had fallen far behind. If she let the trainsman take her, would the thieves hurt Papa?

She set her teeth, ready to consent, but Clay wasn't waiting any longer. He stepped up to the edge and leapt off the platform. He landed squarely in his saddle, the satchel on his shoulder flapping into his lap, and the horse fell back a step to readjust as he gathered his reins.

"Come on!" Clay called, holding out a hand for her.

He was moving as fast as the wind. Sadie clenched her fists and slid her toes up to the edge. Clay turned to check the car behind her, then shouted again.

"You gotta do it now!"

She took a sharp breath, bent her knees, and pushed off the platform. Leaping through the cool air, completely separating herself from the train, seemed like utter insanity. She screamed and cursed herself as she flew, crossing her fingers, praying to the Lord above, and hoping like mad that Clay could snatch her out of the air.

She hit him hard in the chest, and he grunted but managed to get his arms around her. She slid down into the saddle in front of him, legs in the air and arms around his shoulder. Her body rocked and drummed along with the churning hoofbeats below her. She was a mess, but she'd made it. Relief and a wave of thanks washed over her.

It lasted but a moment before she realized her new predicament. Pressed up against a strange man with her legs flailing in the air over one of his arms. Her dress was in disarray, hopefully at least covering her legs. She writhed against his chest.

"Set me straight," she called out.

"Stop bucking around," he grumbled through clenched teeth. "We're fine."

The galloping beats beneath them slowed as Clay veered them away from the train and up onto a grassy hill. The horse fell into a bouncy trot, and Sadie held tighter to the outlaw's chest, cursing him.

They came to a halt on the knoll. Clay adjusted his seat in the saddle and lowered her to the ground. Sadie's boots hit the earth, and she crumpled into the grass. Her heart pounded, and her breath sputtered as she chased to catch it.

She'd never done anything so utterly insane and idiotic in her life. She clutched at handfuls of grass to ground herself. The most danger she'd ever been in was the time that grizzly bear decided it wanted the elk she was hauling in with Papa. That was an easy decision to make though. Give the bear the deer.

The day she and her fiancé Robert had faced off with the vicious lone wolf had been pretty thrilling as well, though nothing as ridiculous as jumping out of a moving train.

She shook her head and took a long breath. Clay's boots hit the ground next to her, followed by hard fingers on her shoulder.

"Are you okay?"

She spun and backed away from the man. "Are you crazy? We just jumped off a train!"

Clay sat back on his heels to stare at her. Then he shook his head and tugged the black mask down his face, revealing a strong square jaw covered in a smooth layer of dark stubble and locks of sandy hair pulled loose beneath his black hat. His lips twisted in an amused smirk.

"I might be crazy, but you did okay. I assume that was your first time."

She narrowed her eyes, trying to follow his words. "What?"

"First time jumping off a train. I've done it a heap of times."

Her wide eyes rolled in disbelief. "Are you trying to get killed?"

"Of course not. But there's danger everywhere."

"But there's no need to invite it."

"You're right. I should just stay home in my slippers and let life pass by my window."

"That's not life going by, blowing its horn. That's a train."

Clay scowled, but the corner of his lips quirked up when he looked at her again.

Sadie rubbed her fingers over her sweaty brow. These fellows were insane. They belonged in a hospital. She wanted to run, but it wasn't as if she could catch the train again. Or get away from the outlaws and their horses.

Hopefully whatever they had in mind for her would be over quickly so she and Papa could be on their way. Before their lives were in danger once again.

Her memory rushed back to the loud pop and the dreadful sight of that man on the train crumbling to the ground. She shuddered. These men meant business, and she didn't want to be on the receiving end of any of their ill decisions.

She'd have to play nice for the time being.

A shrill whistle behind them brought Clay to his feet. The buckskin stomped a hoof, ears on a swivel. Hoofbeats came up the backside of the hill, and Sadie stood as Clay's companion rode up on his black horse. Papa sat astride the beast behind Tom, clutching at the thief's ribs.

"Don't just stand 'round there," Tom said as he yanked his

mask down around his neck. He had the same handsome nose and brush of dark hair on his jaw as Clay, but the angry scowl on his face ruined his look. "Let's get out of here before they stop that train and come after us."

Clay slid the bags behind his saddle and strapped them on. He'd just fitted his boot into the stirrup when something whizzed by. Sadie whipped around with a gasp. A second bullet hit a tree at the edge of the hill, exploding in a spray of wood and a splintered branch. She screamed and hit the ground.

CHAPTER 3

"What the hell?" growled Tom as he pulled his horse around and spurred into a gallop. "Move it, Clay!"

Clay pulled up into his saddle.

Sadie hunched down with her hands over her head. Who was shooting? She spun in a small circle but saw nothing but empty train tracks in the distance and rolling hills moving up and down over the plains. There wasn't a town or a residence in sight. No other people for miles it seemed.

Except for those two men on horses that breached the next hill over. They were headed for them, guns drawn. Sadie coughed through a gasp.

"Quit starin' and get your ass up here," Clay said, circling his horse around and holding out a hand for her.

She didn't need near as much coaxing as before. She slapped her hand into his, and he pulled her up onto the back of his horse. She'd barely had a moment to grab hold before they were off. She clung to Clay's back, eyes pinched shut, trying to imagine she was anywhere else. Not squashed against a stranger with her legs parted and skirts inching up to her knees as she sat astride a galloping horse. Being shot at by marauding outlaws no less.

Robert would be appalled to see her. She tried to put the very idea out of her head. It was a life and death matter. Not a time to worry about being chaste.

"Who is that?" she shouted over the wind and thundering hooves.

"Croakers."

A shudder snaked through her. The heinous crimes of the Croakers were notorious for miles around. She'd wager all of Wyoming knew of the Croakers gang.

Her throat ran dry and moisture sprang to her eyes. Why in all get out were the Croakers after them?

Being shot at was another thing she'd failed to ever encounter. Life in the west was perilous, and everyone had a gun, but she lived in a civilized society. Or at least she did whenever she actually went into town. Nevertheless, no one had taken a shot at her.

"Hang tight," Clay called over his shoulder.

She didn't have time to question him before the horse beneath her crushed through a bed of gravel and hopped over a small stream. She wrapped her arms around Clay's chest and leaned into him as they climbed the opposite bank.

Her father would be shocked to find her so plastered against the strange man, trying not to topple off the back of the horse. Her knees touched the outside of Clay's hips, and she pressed her lips together until they throbbed. How dare he put her in such an inappropriate position.

Yet, she didn't imagine outlaws were known for their class.

They traveled along the edge of the embankment and onto a worn path. Hooves churned the hard dirt. A few gunshots sounded in the distance, and her teeth clenched harder each time.

After what seemed like ages, the horse slowed. Sadie opened her eyes. Her arms and legs ached as they relaxed, and she sat up to look around.

Clay dipped his head as an overhang of trees stretched out to cover them. Tom's black horse was waiting inside the alcove, huffing out loud wet breaths. Sadie blinked wide eyes as she looked the shadowed figure over. Only one man sat upon the horse's back.

She gasped. "Where's my father?"

Tom's face was solid, unforgiving. "He took a bullet. I left him by the river."

A rush of nerves nearly made her vomit. "You left him? But he needs help!"

"He don't need no help where he's at now, lady."

A yelp escaped her lips. "He's—"

"Dead. Gone. No more use to us," Tom grunted.

Another urge to vomit boiled up Sadie's throat, and she pressed her tight lips into Clay's shoulder to stifle another anguished cry.

Dead? How could he be dead? Her eyes burned, and the lump in her throat knotted so hard she couldn't breathe.

They'd just been riding home on the train. Minding their own business. Her fingers began to tremble.

Warm hands covered hers. Clay pressed her fingers into his chest gently.

At first, the touch grounded her, and she wanted to lean into him further and cry. But logic snapped in her brain like a stick across her knee. It was his fault. These men. They'd stolen them for no good reason. Ripped them right off their train and paraded them around in gunfire.

She snatched her hands-free and pushed her palms into Clay's back, fighting to get away from him. She didn't want to touch him at all, the vile murderer.

"No use to us?" she spat. "He was my father!"

Tom glared at her, a dirty snarl on his lips.

She wanted to bite him. She pushed off Clay far enough to swing her leg over the back of his horse and slide down. Her boots rocked as she hit the soft grass, and she nearly lost her footing as she lunged for Tom.

But Clay was on her. His arms wrapped her up from behind, lifting her from the ground and spinning her away from his brother.

"Tom," he growled. "How about a little couth?"

Sadie's vision blurred as she clenched her teeth and struggled against Clay's arms. He hardly even had to squeeze her to hold her still, and she fell hopelessly against him. A new heavier wave of pain hit her, and she forced back the cry of anguish in her throat. It ached as her body constricted in on itself, but she wouldn't show these ruthless men her belly just yet.

A hazy Tom gave a shrug of his shoulder. "I needed him for money, and those damn Croakers just decided to put a bullet in him and steal him right out from under me. How's that for couth?"

Clay shook his head with a grumble.

"Least we still got her," Tom said, jerking his chin in her direction. "Blindfold her and let's get out of here."

"Wait!" Sadie cried, reaching out for him. "We can't just leave him out here. He needs to be buried."

The disgusted wrinkle in Tom's nose made her stomach sink.

"We're going back to camp," he said. "He don't need us anymore."

The outlaw urged his horse forward and rode out from under the trees. Clay loosened his grip on her and pulled in a labored breath as he watched his brother go. Then he turned to Sadie.

She could feel his eyes on her, but she refused to meet

them. The last thing she needed was those endless blue eyes begging her to speak to him. But she had to hold it together.

She wouldn't cry in front of him. She would go about her business, carry out whatever idiotic money-making plan they had, and walk away. They couldn't break her down. Even if they'd taken the only family she had in the world. Her livelihood. And for what? A few coins?

Monsters, all of them.

She stiffened when Clay took her by the arm and helped her onto his horse. After hopping into the saddle, he twisted around to face her, removing the bandana from around his neck and slipping it over her eyes without a word.

Her world went dark. The cloth smelled of leather and sweat. She let it envelop her, the only thing she had left to ground her to reality.

Clay's fingers bumbled against the back of her head as he knotted the bandana. It pulled at her hair but stayed firm over her eyes.

The silence drew out. Neither moved or spoke. Then his hand was on her shoulder. A light tough but enough to make her twitch.

"Sorry about your Pa." His low voice dropped further, nearly a whisper.

She swallowed hard as he turned back in his seat. Then they were moving. She reached out to grab at the edges of his coat to steady herself, but she refused to touch him further.

Her hips rocked with the horse's ambling gait, and she did her best to keep her mind off the events of the evening. They were too hard to swallow. Who would ever expect to get snatched off a moving train and flee from gunmen on horseback? Not to mention being kidnapped by outlaws and losing her father.

As the evening air grew cooler, the anger inside her subsided, and a darkness replaced it. She rested her forehead against Clay's shoulder and wept silently into the bandana on her face.

The pain of losing Papa sliced into her like a knife through butter. The carelessness of it dragged her down into a prickly pit in her chest. As she let the pain seep from her eyes, a new fear replaced it.

Tom had let her father die without a blink of his sharp black eyes. What was he going to do with her?

She sat back, wanting to escape the hard wall of Clay's body. The vile taste in her mouth that had flooded in when she'd heard of Papa's fate returned, and she grimaced.

"Doing okay back there, Sadie?" Clay's voice was low and casual.

It stopped her breath as a new anger boiled within her. "It's Miss Tanner. And I'm not dead yet, so I suppose I'm making do."

She felt him straighten in his seat. "Yeah. I'm real sorry about that, Miss Tanner. I know Tom didn't mean to hurt your Pa. Really, it screwed up his plans." He chuckled but quickly covered it by clearing his throat. "Look, Tom ain't a bad guy, really. He's just got a plan up his sleeves, and then he'll let you go."

"I don't believe that for a second. I saw him shoot that man on the train."

"He does get a little paranoid, but I don't think—"

"Why do you take orders from such a horrible man, anyway?"

"Now, look here, Miss Tanner." His voice had grown hard, and he twisted around. He must have been staring right at her. She clenched her jaw and faced him without a flinch. "Tom might lack the class you got, but he's a good man. He takes care of his family and lays his life on the line for them every day."

"He seems like a bossy hothead to me. Why do you let him just order you around like that?"

Clay settled back in the saddle without a word. After a few breaths, she considered prodding him again, but his voice drifted back in the cool breeze.

"I always have. He's my brother."

Any retort she had absolved on her tongue, and she fell silent. But the calm was brief.

"We're here," Clay said.

The insect buzzing and first chirps of evening crickets faded into the sounds of civilization. People talking and moving about. The crackling of a fire. Horses greeting one another. A few random chords on a guitar.

At first, her heart leapt. She would be saved! But when Clay removed her blindfold, she found herself in a campsite in the middle of a clearing in the forest. Lines of tents curled around a big central fire where a few people sat, one toying with a guitar. Horses grazed beyond the edge of the tents. Other people were scattered about the campsite.

Hovering at the edge of one of the larger tents, Tom stood with his hands shoved in his pockets. He watched them like a hawk, unmoving, and Sadie's nerves stirred.

"Come on down. It's okay."

Clay had dismounted and was standing beneath her, offering a hand to help her down. She stared at him for a moment, eyes narrowing a fraction, then slid off the other side of the horse. She teetered for a heartbeat and swung her arms wide to steady herself. By the time Clay came around to face her, she stood with her arms crossed over her chest.

"Now what?" she spat. There was no way she was going to make this easy for them.

"Now I have to go have a word with Tom." He took her by the elbow and herded her toward the center of camp. She resisted, but his fingers were strong on her arm. "I want you to take a seat by the fire and warm up."

She eyed the people gathered around the fire pit. A man held a guitar. The other two were women. Nerves clenched in her stomach. There were other captors already? She pulled against Clay's grasp. "I don't know those people. You can't leave me with them," she hissed.

Clay looked down at her as he pulled her along. "You don't know me either. Might as well make a new friend."

"I don't want a new friend. I want—" She shut her mouth as she breached the fire-sitters' circle. They looked up at her in surprise.

A woman dressed in brown trousers with a bushel of long blonde hair put her hands on her hips. She lifted an eyebrow at Clay with a grin. "Bringing them home now, are you?"

He let Sadie's arm go. "Ain't bringing no one home. Tom's wrapping up a deal with this one."

The blonde's eyebrows bounced with a wide grin. "A deal, huh? About time he figured himself out."

Clay shook his head with a hand toss. "No, not like that. A money deal."

"Oh, they're all money deals, honey."

Clay grunted, but this time with a smile. He nodded toward the blonde, a soft hand landing on Sadie's arm. "That's Clara. She can get you something to eat. That's Ginny and Jack."

Ginny was a petite young woman with long, loose chest-nut-colored locks. She grinned at Sadie. "Hey there."

Next to her Jack adjusted the guitar on his lap to give Sadie a one finger salute. His eyes were hazy, and his mouth turned up in a lopsided greeting. She imagined the bottle of whiskey propped next to the stump he sat on was to thank for his droopy expression.

"I'll be back," Clay said as he departed.

Sadie watched his hand on her arm slip away and shivered at the chill its absence left behind.

"Are you cold?" Clara asked, voice laced with an Irish lilt. She beckoned her closer to the fire. "I've got an extra plate of food here if you're hungry."

Sadie glanced over her shoulder at Clay as he strode away. The last streams of fading light filtering through the tree limbs lit up his broad back and the cowboy hat that sat low on his head. He joined Tom and headed into the large tent. When her gaze returned to the fire, Sadie realized Clara was staring at her.

"Oh, no food. Thank you," Sadie murmured as she moved closer and sat on a short stool.

With the twists in her stomach that evening, she doubted she'd ever eat again.

"It's there when you want it. Welcome to camp, by the way." The woman wiped her hand on her pants and offered it around the fire. "Clara McGowen."

Sadie stared at the hand a moment. She'd never been offered a handshake by a woman before. Much less a woman in the middle of an outlaw hideout. Neither of the women she'd met seemed to be under duress though. Confusion and questions clouded her brain.

She waited a beat before placing her fingers in the awaiting palm. "Sadie Tanner."

Clara grinned and grasped what little Sadie offered. "Pleased to meet you."

"Surely," Sadie said, glancing at her company again before clearing her throat. "I can't say I ever imagined what it would be like inside the hideout of a ruthless gang, but I can say I never expected to see any women."

Clara snorted a laugh out the side of her mouth as she leaned forward toward the fire. "Guess men ain't the only people who run from the law."

"You mean you—"

"Some of us have done things we may not be particularly proud of, yes. But we're still living and surviving like anyone else."

The thought of living among the ill-reputed and murderers made Sadie's stomach turn. There was no place for them in society. They deserved to live out in the forest with the animals.

Even if Clara's smile was warm, and her laughter alluring.

"I love your dress, Sadie." Ginny's voice broke through the soft crackle of the fire. "I'm going to get me something pretty like that one day."

"Thank you."

Ginny wore a threadbare cotton dress that was missing half the lace across the low-dipping neckline. A faded lilac that might have been handsome in its time, it looked like it might fall slap off one day soon.

"I like that dress you wear, Ginny," the man next to her drawled.

Sadie lifted an eyebrow at the way he grinned at her. She was sure he did like that dress. Any man would.

"I know you do, Jackie." Ginny smiled at him through her eyelashes and gave him a wink.

He laughed. She rolled up to her feet, bending and gliding through the air like a serpent trying to hypnotize its prey. His droopy eyes were wide open, and Ginny blew him a kiss. He slung his guitar off his lap and lunged for her. She squealed and frolicked away, swaying man in tow.

Sadie blinked in utter confusion. What had just happened?

Clara snickered nearby. "Don't mind Ginny. She's as sweet as they come, but she drives them boys crazy."

Sadie jerked her head around to look at her remaining source of company. "Where'd they go?"

One of the blonde's eyebrows peaked. "Off to play, I'd reckon. Don't rightly want to know. Do you?"

Sadie's nose wrinkled, and she averted her eyes, staring into the fire. "No, that's a private matter."

"Not much privacy around here. Speaking of which, do you know what you're doing here?"

"Something about money." Sadie shrugged. "I didn't get all the details. We were too busy trying not to die."

Clara grimaced. "Isn't it always the way? Trying to have a meaningful conversation and something dangerous comes along. I'm guessing Tom's got something up his sleeve. He's always got some new plan hatching."

"He must have plenty of money then."

"Well, they don't always pan out quite like he wants, but it's expensive to keep this family afloat too. I guess we could all use a bit more money. Well, maybe not you."

Sadie frowned and glanced down at her dress. Her mother's dress that had hung in the closet for years. She didn't quite fill it out like her, but it seemed the most appropriate thing to wear to town for Papa's interview. She'd own a dozen more like them if she could.

"I don't have a dollar to my name, Miss McGowen."

"Please, call me Clara. I'm sorry to hear that, but I can sympathize. Although today I am happy to say that I have two." She whipped two dollar bills from her pocket and waved them in the firelight with a grin.

Sadie's lips twitched. Clara's good nature calmed her nerves. She found herself relaxing by the warm fire, enjoying the woman's company.

Until Tom barked her name.

CHAPTER 4

Sadie stared at Tom across the campsite. He was rigid, arms crossed over his chest. Clay stood half-inside the tent next to him, backlit by a warm orange light, but she could still make his eyes out in the shadows.

"Need you over here," Tom called out again.

His tone grated against her fragile nerves. She clenched her fingers as dread balled up in her gut like dead weight.

"I think you'll be alright," Clara said in a hushed tone. She'd shifted closer and was watching the men across the campsite as well. "Those boys are rowdy, but Ace keeps them respectful."

"Ace?"

Clara nodded her head in the direction of the tent. Sadie bit into her lower lip, considering her options.

She could turn tail, run out of the campsite, and hope they had a lousy shot, but that seemed like quite the risky venture surrounded by outlaws. She could swipe a gun and threaten them until they let her go, except there didn't seem to be any weapons close by that weren't strapped to someone's person. Or she could hold her head up high, march over to the waiting men, and pretend not a bit of her kidnapping bothered her.

She really wanted to take Option A and high tail it.

But doing as they wanted was the safest option.

She got to her feet, and Clara followed her, tugging at her elbow.

"I'll be right out here. If you need help, just shout," she said.

"Thank you, Clara."

The women exchanged tight-lipped smiles, and Sadie stepped out of the fire circle and headed across the grass.

A man wearing a white hat stood alongside a parked wagon nearby, watching as she moved. A woman with curly red hair appeared behind him, peeking out at her from behind his elbow. Another man hovered near the edge of the big tent where Tom and Clay waited.

Sadie steeled her nerves. She was surrounded by outlaws. Vermin who would kill her the moment they had the chance.

At least that's what she had thought before. Except Clara was warm and friendly. Ginny seemed friendly enough. But they were women.

It was the men that were closing in around her.

Her skin itched as she neared Tom. Everything inside her screamed to get out of there. Was it too late for Option A? Because it was definitely sounding like the right one.

"Pick up your feet," Tom grumbled, giving her an impatient knuckle in the shoulder. "Ace can't wait to meet you."

She rolled her shoulder out of his finger with a wince and stomped into the tent flaps. Clay stood waiting without a sound. Those shadowed blue eyes found hers for an instant. They were soft, much unlike his brother's. It pulled some of the fear and frustration from her body, and she walked into the tent with a lighter step.

Drab white sheets of canvas stretched across the wooden

post frames of the box tent. A few photos and newspaper clippings were lit on the walls by an orange lantern sitting on a small nightstand in the corner. A cot draped with furs stood next to it. The man sitting on the edge of the bed stood as she entered.

Ace was a tall man, lean and trim beneath a pair of black pants and red suspenders. His dark hair curled around his ears beneath his black hat, and he looked impeccably clean. Face smooth but for the neatly trimmed patch of hair on his chin and a pair of cufflinks at his wrists. He held out a hand and offered her a seat in a small wooden armchair across from his bed.

"Miss Tanner. Welcome to our camp. I hope you have been well taken care of." She caught the quick dart of his eyes, a twitch in his eyebrow, as he gave Tom a glance.

"I appreciate your welcome, sir, but I—"

"Excuse me. My apologies, my lady. I should have introduced myself. How rude of me." He swept a hand across his middle as he tipped into a short bow. "I am Ace Van den Berg, and I am the head of this family."

She'd read about a local gang in the newspapers. They'd been stirring up trouble in Emerald Falls for the last several months. The thought of dangerous outlaws made her squirm in both anxiety and anger over their careless actions toward her town.

Ace continued to smile, oblivious to her discomfort. He motioned toward the front of the tent. "I'm sure you've already met the Pearson boys here."

Tom didn't move when she looked his way, but Clay tipped the edge of his hat. It covered his eyes for a heartbeat, and they seemed to sparkle a brighter blue upon their return. She stared. The lantern light flickered across his face and the small quirk in the corner of his mouth.

"Most informally, yes," she murmured, then back to Ace, "I

was stolen, you know. Robbed right off my train. Then shoved into a gunfight. Where I lost my father." Her throat seized, and she clenched her fist, refusing to cry. Not now. Not in front of these insensitive men that could care less about the death of her father or how lost she felt without him. "Whatever idiotic scheme your boys have cooked up, I can assure you it was not worth all that."

Ace steepled his fingers against his lips and took his seat once more. His brow furrowed as he drew in a long breath. "My apologies, Miss Tanner, and you are right. It wasn't worth all that trouble. Your father's death is a horrible tragedy. Hurting you was not intended."

"Then what is your intention?"

He turned and slipped a sheet of paper from the drawer of his nightstand and handed it to her. "Are you related to the Tanners over in St. Aspen?"

Sadie stared at Ace, frozen. It wasn't a question she'd been ready for. She hadn't seen that part of her family in nearly a decade, despite living so close. No one ever brought them up. Especially Papa.

Ace doing so made her stomach feel queer.

Unsure whether the truth would be safer than not, she went with it. "Yes."

His stoic and friendly face didn't change, only moved an inch up and down as he nodded. Though she thought she could discern a slight twinkle in his eye.

"We best let someone know you're safe then."

"Aunt Hilda?" Sadie lifted a shoulder with a wrinkle of her nose. "I don't think she—"

"She most certainly would want to know that you're in the company of a group living outside the law. She'll do whatever it takes to get you back. Don't you think?"

In truth, she wasn't sure her Aunt Hilda would even remember her name, much less care what company she was keeping. Something about Ace's words, however, set her teeth on edge. Tricky schemes were afoot.

"I would hope she would, yes," she said. That part was true, but she wouldn't hold her breath over it.

Ace nodded. "As would I. As would us all. I think your lovely Aunt Hilda would be willing to part with a little money to keep you safe from harm."

Realization hit Sadie like a slap on the wrist. How had she not realized earlier?

She glanced over at the men hovering just inside the tent flap. Tom leaned against a wooden crate, a smug look on his face. Clay studied the twill rug. It was one time she was happy not to see those deep blue eyes. She didn't want to see the truth in them.

"You're holding me for ransom?" she snapped, popping her eyes back to Ace.

He showed her his palms, leaning back with a crooked grin that made her skin crawl. "We ain't causing any trouble now, Miss Tanner. From what I hear your aunty has more than enough money to share a bit, especially if it's to see that you are returned safely. We don't have to tell her you're not really in any trouble, do we?" He gave her a wink.

Her lip twitched, and she leaned back in her chair to put a larger space between her and the snake of a gang leader. She wanted to yell at him, remind him that she most certainly had been in danger already. Her father had been killed, for Lord's sake. Now she was surrounded by a whole camp of thieving, dirty outlaws who would do who knew what to her. She held the shudder down low in her spine, refusing to show him her fear.

"Of course not. I'm sure she'll send the money soon," she said with the most stoic face she could muster.

She knew she was lying through her teeth, but something told her her life might depend on that lie.

Ace's grin grew, and her fingers relaxed around the edge of her seat.

"Perfect. We appreciate your cooperation, Miss Tanner," he said as he got to his feet. "Have you met Miss McGowen? Lovely blonde in charge of the food out there? Take that paper on out to her, and she'll help you write a letter to your Aunt Hilda. We'll make sure all that gets taken care of right away."

Sadie stared at the paper in her hand as she stood to follow him out of the tent. She was going to write her own ransom note. For some dirty train robber. She couldn't believe the reality she'd landed herself in.

Ace's men stepped out of the way as he departed the tent. Sadie followed, shivering as the crisp air enveloped her. The sun had gone down quickly, replacing the chilly breeze with encroaching winter cold.

"You take care of that," Ace said, waving a hand toward the center campfire. "Then my boys here will get you set up for the night. Let me know if you need anything, Miss Tanner." He made a production of sweeping his arm out in front of him in a bow with a grin she couldn't quite read. "Enjoy your stay at the Van den Berg camp."

Her teeth gnawed into her inner cheek, biting back a retort. Enjoy her stay? She was being held prisoner! Her fist clenched at her side as she watched the outlaw stride away.

Then someone stepped up behind her and touched her elbow. She jumped, jerking away from the cold fingers on her skin.

"Welcome to Hotel de Van den Berg," Tom sniggered. "I'm sure the Tanner family will be delighted to pay us fine gentlemen for keeping you safe. We are heroes, after all."

The fringe of his jacket smelled of fish and vinegar. She grimaced and turned her head away.

"You know, we ain't got much room for hoity-toity ladies

around here," he spat. She could almost feel the heat radiating off of him and was afraid to look back. "You best find a way to get comfortable tonight, because there ain't no down pillows and feet warmers in any of these tents."

Tom brushed past her and stomped off. She listened for his boots to get a few yards away before she glanced after him. He walked past the couple that'd watched her go in, the white hat tipping as the man spoke. She couldn't hear what he said, but Tom whipped a hand in the air angrily. The pair looked at her, and she withdrew, her cheeks burning.

"His bark is worse than his bite."

The deep voice behind her made her breath catch. She'd forgotten about Clay.

He stepped up on her opposite side, hands deep in his pockets and hat low over his eyes.

"I'm not so sure," she said. "He killed two men today."

The blue eyes caught hers. "Your father was not his fault."

"He was in his care."

Clay's jaw set. "It's a dangerous world out here."

"It wasn't a dangerous world on that train. We would have been perfectly safe if you'd left us alone."

His jaw rolled under, and his nostrils flared, but he had no reply. She tilted her chin defiantly, hands resting on her hips.

"We best get to Clara to help with that letter," he said after a moment. "It's getting late."

Sadie tucked the sheet of paper against the soft folds of her dress and made her way over to the fire pit without another word, leaving Clay to trail behind.

Clara was spooning chopped vegetables from a pot near the fire into a metal bowl. When she saw Sadie returning, her face lit up.

"Sadie, back in one piece I see." She grinned, though Sadie was unsure of the comment. Her face must have said so. "I'm just kiddin'. I told you Ace was a pretty nice guy. I've never seen him harm a woman."

Sadie bit back an angry reply and held out the blank paper. "I need to write a ransom note."

Clara stood and propped her hands on her hips. "Oh, dear. I'm sorry. But hey, that's the least violent trick they pull."

"They killed my father."

Clara's face turned green, and she glanced at Clay who was already holding out a hand in his own defense.

"It was Croakers. An accident."

The blonde's shoulders slumped, and her eyes welled with sympathy. "Oh, Sadie. I'm so sorry."

A lump caught in Sadie's throat.

"I'll survive."

"I know you will," Clara said. "You look like a strong girl. In the meantime, why don't you let me take care of this for you?" She slipped the paper from Sadie's hand with a gentle smile. "Don't worry about this anymore. Get you some sleep."

"Thank you."

Clay tapped a couple fingers to Sadie's elbow. "This way. I'll show you where you can rest."

She wanted to refuse and park herself next to the fire with Clara, where it was safe and warm. The breeze was growing frigid, whipping up her short sleeves and biting her feet. She shivered.

Clay's fingers tugged at her. Gentle but insistent. She couldn't read his face, but it seemed silly to push her luck. She stepped out of the warm fire circle and followed him.

"It's too cold out here to be sleeping on the ground," she murmured.

"We don't haul beds around. The ground will suffice."

"Ace has a bed. What of that?"

Clay coughed out a laugh. "Ace has a wagon. He can carry

around a bed if he wants."

"Why don't you have a wagon?"

His eyes cut over to her for a moment before focusing on their path again. "I don't have enough things to warrant a wagon. I don't need it."

"A bed seems kind of important, don't you think?"

He lifted a shoulder as he stepped up to the opening of a blue-cloth tent, covered on three sides. "It's just a place to sleep."

Sadie stepped up next to him. A small stack of blankets sat on the deer hide stretched over the grass. "That's where I'm sleeping? I'll freeze."

Clay grabbed the blankets and spread one over the fur. "I'm going to start a fire out there," he jabbed a thumb over his shoulder as he added another blanket to her pallet. A small charcoal circle filled with the remains of an old fire sat in the center of the surrounding three tents. "You have plenty of blankets. I'm sure we can find more if we need to. You'll be just fine."

"But I'm not properly dressed to sleep out here. I don't have sleeves like you. Nor boots high enough to keep my ankles warm. It's too late in the autumn to be sleeping outdoors. Once the elk start moving—"

"I'll take care of it." He shook his head with a scowl as he shoved the remaining blanket into her hands and stepped out of the tent. "You city girls are all the same. Lord forbid you get your hands dirty or spend a few hours away from your fireplaces and your crochet."

"Excuse me," Sadie scoffed, throwing the blanket onto the pallet. "I am not—"

"I said I'll build the fire," he said, voice loud and stern.

She hesitated, remembering who she was dealing with.

"You won't die out here," he continued in a quieter tone. "We haven't."

CHAPTER 5

The pop of a gunshot catapulted Sadie off the ground the next morning. She sat up like a spring, jerking her head left and right in alarm.

The first thing she noticed was that she was outside, covered on three sides by a sheet of cloth. Sunlight twinkled through the thin fabric.

The Van den Berg campsite.

The previous day's events came crashing down on her, and she rubbed a hand over her sore, swollen eyes and chapped face. She'd spent the better part of the night quietly mourning the loss of her father. He'd been stripped away so quickly, she could still hardly believe it.

People living on the edge of the western wilderness were no strangers to the loss of loved ones. She was lucky they'd remained safe for so long, especially living apart from the town as they did.

Being left to fend for herself in that world was still a hard pill to swallow.

Another gunshot went off, and she jumped with a gasp.

She clutched at the red wool blanket in her lap and threw it around her shoulders as she stumbled out of the tent.

The mid-morning sun hit her square in the face, and she balked, shading her eyes with a blanketed arm. A few people lingered at the central campfire. A few more stood at the edge of camp just a few tents away. Tom was among them.

He lifted a revolver in the air and fired off another round. His two companions fell into a fit of laughter. One of them, a grizzled old man with a shaggy white beard, pointed into the field nearby. Sadie stood on tiptoe and strained to see what he was looking at.

For a moment she saw nothing in the swaying green grass. Trees waved in the morning breeze. The field appeared empty.

Then a red fox leapt into the air just twenty yards from the men, clearing the grass and twisting around with a yip. Its head popped back as it was yanked to the ground, and it bucked about in a fit of panic. Its leg must have been snagged in a trap.

For some reason, the men found it hilarious.

A fire boiled her insides, and she clenched her teeth. With her hands on her hips, she marched toward the group of ignoramuses.

A hand on her shoulder stopped her.

She wheeled around to find Clara hovering behind her.

"I wouldn't mess with them." The blonde watched the group of men with sharp eyes. "Just saying. Not all the men around here are as nice as others."

"But they're torturing that creature," Sadie scoffed.

"They're not shooting at him. They just like to watch him dance around." Clara's voice lowered, and she crossed her arms over her chest. "They're little more than children, some of these men. Toddlers with guns are more dangerous than real men." She cracked a grin that was both amused and sad.

Sadie wondered how long Clara had been putting up with the gang's horrible men. And why.

She shook her head and looked for the fox again. The tip of his ears breached the grass. He must have been lying down. Probably exhausted.

Her father used traps in his hunting. She thought it was inhumane and unfair. He'd lectured plenty on upkeeping their business and that the traps were necessary, but when she sat on a pile of raccoon pelts on the way to market, she never felt like it was a fair trade.

But she did like to eat and sleep indoors, so she avoided questioning her father's practices.

"Too bad it ain't a deer," Clara said with a half-smile. "We're running low on meat."

"You trap deer?" Sadie asked.

"We don't trap them, no. But we hunt them." Clara's nose wrinkled. "You're not one of those greens only girls, are you? I mean, I can get you a bowl of vegetables, but most of them go into the pot with the meat, and I don't—"

Sadie held up a hand. "I'm not. I eat plenty of deer. I just don't like the idea of snagging them first. It seems unfair. Especially if they're going to be gawked at like that." She sneered at the backs of the laughing men.

"No one uses traps as far as I know. Just a good rifle. I think you're turning green. Here, I'll handle this." Clara put a hand on Sadie's arm as she strode past.

Loose waves of blonde sashayed behind her back as she marched up to Tom and his friends.

"Hey, Pearson. Ace needs a word with you. He seemed a little steamed up about that crate of beer you brought in. Didn't break one did you?"

Tom's face skewed in annoyance. "I checked them all. Ain't a broken bottle in there. I only jostled the crate a little." He holstered his gun and stalked into camp with a growl.

His two companions followed like bewildered puppies.

Clara flashed a grin at Sadie, who felt a renewed warmth in her chest. Maybe not all outlaws were bad. She joined the woman on the edge of camp and peered out into the grass. Two trembling ears still topped the green blades.

"Be careful," Clara warned, holding out a small knife. "A trapped animal can be vicious."

"Rightfully so," Sadie murmured as she took the tool and stepped into the field.

She'd seen her father deal with snared animals a hundred times. A fox was just a kitten compared to a badger, but it could still cause some serious damage. Of course, her father's intent had always been to kill the captor. She had the opposite in mind.

Fitting the dull edge of the blade in her teeth, she swept the blanket off her shoulders, cradled it against her body, and grasped both corners.

The fox didn't stir as she neared it. As the rest of the creature's body came into view, Sadie's pulse pounded in her head.

The sharp gold eyes turned up at her. His body went rigid for half a second before he leapt to his feet, but she was prepared. She pounced on him, trapping him beneath the outstretched cloth.

What she wasn't prepared for, however, was how much fight he still had left him in. He writhed and bucked against her body. A head clunk to the chin, a powerful foot in the chest. Once, he nearly wiggled his head out of one side of her net, but she managed to close it back around him.

"Stop," she pleaded through clenched teeth.

The snare peg was just a foot away. If she could settle him down, she could cut the cord. It would be much too dangerous for the both of them to do it if he got free.

After another two wild bucks, his body pressed low to the

ground, and he stopped. Sadie froze, waiting, but nothing else happened. She smiled around the dull edge of the knife and slid it out of her mouth. As she leaned over to press it into the rope, the fox jumped up again. The blanket exploded in a fury of yowls and kicks beneath her.

She sawed the knife into the rope furiously.

But she wasn't quick enough.

Snapping jaws sprang loose of the blanket and pinned her arm. Teeth sank into the tender flesh underneath her forearm, and she yelped. The fox darted from her grasp and leapt away. The rope pulled taut for an instant before popping free. Red tail swirling over the top of the grass, he sprinted across the field into the trees beyond.

Sadie sat back with a sigh and checked her arm. Small drops of blood had gathered on her pale skin, but the wound was superficial. He'd only tagged her.

"Are you okay?" Clara called as she jogged up.

"I'm fine," Sadie said, smoothing out her dress and plucking the knife from the ground.

Clara offered a hand and pulled Sadie to her feet.

"At least he got away," the blonde said. "That was a nice thing you did."

"Pretty stupid if you ask me," came a deep drawl behind them.

They turned to find Clay crossing the grass at the edge of camp.

"Wild animals will destroy your day," he continued. "It's best to leave them alone."

"I seem to have a softer spot than normal for caged animals today," Sadie said with a perk of an eyebrow.

He regarded her for a moment, then nodded his head to her arm. "Didn't help you much, did it?"

She glanced down at the wound. The skin was turning

red, and it was beginning to sting, but the bleeding had stopped.

"Sometimes helping others hurts. I had to do something."

Clara cleared her throat. "She was just heading Tom and his goons off before they did something cruel." The way she looked pointedly at Clay made Sadie's stomach turn. "Speaking of heroes, I need a favor, Clay."

He rested his hands on his hips. "Another one?"

"Don't play like that lamb and potatoes you brought back was for me. I just cooked it. You're the one that wanted to eat it."

He rolled his head into a side nod. "Fine. What do you need?"

"Meat. We're running low. Ace sent Jack and Mason out to Emerald Falls this morning. You know Tom and Otis will take all day, and they're not clean shots."

Sadie's pulse flickered, and she drew in a breath. Outlaws in Emerald Falls. It'd been a quiet place until the last couple of years. More and more strangers had been showing up and causing trouble.

Or at least so she'd heard. She didn't frequent town that much and had only witnessed one robbery since the most recent trouble started.

It was odd seeing the crimes from the other side.

"Sure, Clara. I'll go out now and bring you back something. You, come with me," Clay said, pointing at Sadie as he walked back into the tents.

"Miss Tanner. I have a name," she said as she followed. She wanted to protest going along hunting with him. More shooting made her stomach queasy. Especially when she could easily be the next victim.

Reducing her number of captors from a whole gang to one, however, sounded quite promising.

"Right, Miss Tanner. Name's Clay Pearson, by the way. I don't know if we were ever—"

"I gathered."

He nodded stiffly, then continued on through camp. "Can you ride?"

She frowned. "I beg your pardon?"

"Ride. You know, horses."

Annoyed disbelief tickled its way up her throat. "Can't everyone?"

His eyebrows popped, and he shook his head. "You'd be surprised. I've met some girls—"

"Clay, she can stay with me if you'd rather go alone," Clara offered, trailing them along the path through camp.

"Thanks. I can keep an eye on her," he said, coming to a stop and facing the women.

"There's food to prep. Clothes to wash. She'd have plenty to do."

Sadie looked between the two of them with narrowed eyes. She'd never been fought over before. The fact that they were holding her prisoner made it much less thrilling.

"She can help you as soon as we return," Clay said. "I don't think letting her hang around camp is the safest thing for her." When his eyes caught hers, the deep blue was back. No longer the sharp gaze that made her wince, but the dark pools that drew her in. And a deep voice that tickled her insides in odd ways. "I can protect her."

CHAPTER 6

Sadie had spent most of her life not feeling protected. Between her father insisting they live in the forest beyond town, full of bears, cougars, and wolves, and her fiancé Robert cowering at the sight of the wolf on the edge of town that day, she'd had to carry the responsibility of keeping herself alive and unharmed all on her own.

Of course, she'd let herself get captured by the Van den Berg gang, but at least she was still surviving.

When Clay'd declared he had to protect her, she'd been quite intrigued. She'd spent the majority of their trek into the woods staring at his back, broad shoulders cloaked in a faded brown leather jacket. The gray mare beneath her plodded along after Clay's buckskin without a care in the world, leaving Sadie to stare and replay his words in her head.

She wasn't sure why he felt the need to protect her, but the outing with just the two of them was exactly what she needed to get away. She had a much better chance of giving just one man the slip.

"I know a good hill for deer this time of day," Clay said. His voice was low and calm. They must be close.

He steered his horse off the game path, and Sadie's horse followed. The sparsely grown trees thickened. The canopy above became so dense that the sun struggled to break through, and the world below was cloaked in a warm shadow. Even early in the autumn season, some of the leaves had already begun to turn to ocher. Stiff brown leaves sprinkled the ground and crackled under the horses' hooves.

She watched Clay's body move back and forth with ease in the saddle. He'd certainly be difficult to outrun if she was caught. A rifle in a leather sheath protruded from the saddle in front of his knee, and a pair of revolvers were strapped to his hips.

Her lips pinched together as she looked him over. Running from Clay could be more dangerous than she'd considered. He was probably an ace with all those guns, and it wouldn't be anything to kill off a random girl like her.

The thought brought more curiosity than she cared to admit, and she broke the silence with a quiet question.

"Have you killed a lot of people?"

Clay's shoulders flexed, and he turned to glance over his shoulder at her.

"What?"

"You know, being an outlaw and all. How many men have you killed?"

The hard edge of his jaw sharpened as he looked forward again. "Only the ones that shoot at me first."

She blinked, tilting her head. "I've heard a lot of stories of gun-happy outlaws."

He grunted, what could have been a dark laugh. "Me too. That's not really us. We stir up some chaos sometimes, but it's not what we're after. We're just in a rut right now."

"Excuse me?"

"This thieving stuff was never meant to be a full-time gig. We're just trying to make enough to survive. As soon as we have what we need, we'll be gone."

"It sounds like you've been causing a lot of trouble. When can we expect you gone?"

He fell silent with another flex of his jaw.

After a moment, he spoke. "All the deals we make may not be the most honest ones, but we don't set out to hurt people. We have a family to protect too. Once they all have what they need to survive proper, we'll be done."

When she cleared her throat to speak again, he held a palm up at her. Then he pressed a finger to his lips. She closed her mouth with an irritated huff.

Clay stopped next to a row of bushes at the foot of an incline and dismounted.

"I'm going to go farther up this hill and get a couple shots off," he whispered. "You stay back here with Georgene and keep quiet."

Sadie frowned down at him from atop her saddle. "Georgene?"

She nearly missed the small grin that played across Clay's face as he lowered his head, disappearing beneath his hat. His hand slid up the thickly muscled neck of the buckskin mare, and he gave her an affectionate pat.

"Sure. Georgene. She's the best horse in all of Wyoming. She'll keep you safe down here."

Sadie's brow perked, as much at his odd shift into a proud cowboy as the notion that his horse could somehow protect her. "That's good to know. What of this one?" She leaned over to run her fingers through the coarse white mane of the gray horse beneath her. "No super strengths or fancy names?"

Clay looked back up at her. The amused twinkle in his eye caught her further off guard.

"She may not measure up to Georgene, but that's a good horse. She joined us just a couple months ago. I think they've been calling her Clover. Don't worry, if anything happens, she'll stick with Georgene. I'll be back."

With a wink, he pulled a rifle from his saddle and slipped up the gradual incline of the foothill. Sadie crossed her arms over her chest, watching him go. His love for his horse shocked her, and while she wanted to believe his bragging on the beast, she couldn't help but think she'd be much safer in the forest with him around. Even if he was an outlaw. A gun offered much more protection than a horse.

She huffed out a sigh, only a moment before noticing the second gun strapped into the other side of his saddle. Another rifle.

Suddenly she remembered her true objective: to escape. She didn't need an escort as much as she needed a weapon.

She slid down out of her saddle, moving as quietly as she could manage. Her fingers closed around the second rifle's wooden stock, and it slid free from its leather cuff. It was heavy, fully loaded, but nothing she hadn't held before. Usually, her job was to hang back at the house and help tan the hides after Papa brought them home, but she'd gone on plenty of hunting trips and brought in her fair share of skinnable carcasses.

Clay was nearing the top of the hill. He would go up there, maybe over, and be preoccupied with hunting deer. Hopefully, he would get a few good ones for Clara. Sadie liked her, and she wished the woman well, despite being stuck in a hang of lawbreakers.

Once Clay was busy, Sadie could slip off in the other direction. Taking the horse would be too loud, so she'd have to go on foot. It was risky, especially since he'd be on horseback once he noticed she was gone, but it was her only shot.

She stood between the horses and watched as he reached

the hilltop and crept out into the sunlight beyond the tree line. He stood still, and his head moved only a fraction as he scanned the fields beyond the hill.

"So long," she breathed before creeping away.

But a footstep not far off made her freeze.

Crunching brown leaves in the distance drew her eye. Thirty yards through the trees and brush she saw the long thin limbs of a deer. The large spread of antlers on his head caught and tugged at low hanging branches. He was large and magnificent, enough to feed the camp for a few days at least. It was too bad Clay'd gone in the other direction.

The stag continued on through the trees. It glanced at the horses a time or two but didn't seem bothered by them. Sadie hovered in between the beasts, hoping to conceal herself. As the months grew cooler, the stags got more aggressive. She didn't want to tousle with him in her escape and preferred it if he looked past her altogether.

It plodded along past the horses and further away. An empty ache clenched her stomach. She was both hungry and disappointed that Clay wasn't going to be able to bring the monster back to Clara. If only she could alert him somehow without scaring the deer away. Or bringing Clay back down the hill and spoiling her escape attempt.

He'd just have to make do on his own.

A loud crack in the air made her jump. The stag jolted to a stop and lifted his head high, huge ears pointed straight up and pressed forward.

Clay cursed from up on the hill, and she winced silently. Whatever he'd been tracking down below, it sounded as if he'd missed.

Leaves and brush rustled from up high, and the stag's muscles quivered. He was drawn up tighter than a longbow, big black eyes trained on the hilltop.

Sadie wasn't sure if he could see Clay yet, but it wouldn't be long. Then he'd be gone. A horrible missed opportunity.

Without a second thought, she pulled the rifle at her side up and fit it into her shoulder. She rested a hand and the barrel of the gun along the back of Georgene's saddle and lined up the sights with the deer's flexed torso muscles.

Next to her, Clover blew out a breath, and one of the deer's ear popped around. His head shifted. If he saw her, he'd be gone.

She pulled the trigger.

The pop echoed in her ears. Both horses threw up their heads with shrill whinnies. She had to sidestep a couple stomping hooves.

"Miss Tanner?" Clay's boots crashed through the brush further up the hill.

The rifle dropped down to her side again, and she sighed. Her head start had vanished. There was no way she could run from him now and expect to get away.

She should have left the hunting to him. Surely he'd have found some meat eventually. She curled her lip at her impulse decision. Stupid deer.

"Miss Tanner?" Clay called again, much closer.

She peered out from beneath Clover's neck as she rubbed a hand over the dingy fur.

Clay's face was pale, skewed in concern, as he pushed through the last few low hanging branches that separated them. As he drew closer, his brow furrowed, eyes darting around the trees and horses.

"What happened?" he panted.

She held up the rifle with a guilty tilt to her lips. "I shot the deer."

His frown deepened, and he stood silently for an instant, sheer confusion crossing his eyes.

"That was you that shot?" he sputtered.

She fit the rifle to her shoulder again, aiming the barrel into the trees, and racked a cartridge through the mechanism. An unused bullet ejected and hit the leaves at her feet.

"It was me," she said.

"I didn't know you—I mean, I wasn't expecting you to handle guns."

Obviously, since he'd left her with one. She could have just as easily crept up the hill after him and blown him away.

The same realization must have come to him too, because prickles of sweat dotted his hairline, and his eyes rarely left her hands on the gun.

"I've gone hunting a time or two," she said, sliding the rifle back into its sheath on Clay's saddle.

More like a hundred times.

"Wait, wait," Clay said, holding up a hand. "You said you shot a deer?"

Sadie pointed over Georgene's back, then tiptoed through the leaves in the direction she'd shot. "Over here."

She hadn't seen if she'd hit the deer or not, but she led the way to where she'd last seen it.

"My Lord," Clay murmured. "That thing's a beast."

She stared at the stag, on the ground no further than where he'd last stood. Even if she'd ruined her chance to run, she'd be able to bring the meat back to Clara. The woman would be so happy.

A smile formed on Sadie's lips.

"Well, I don't think I easily surprise, Miss Tanner," Clay said as he removed his hat and ran his hand through his hair. The soft-looking strands parted and slid through his fingers, and a strange sensation came over her. She wanted to move her fingers through the sandy locks and determine if they were indeed as soft as they appeared. He placed his hat back on his head and looked at her. She jerked her eyes back down to his face. "But that's a damn good shot, and this will definitely help our low rations."

A puff of pride swelled in her chest, and she nodded. "I'm glad I could help."

Clay hooked his thumbs in his belt and regarded her with a lowered hat, his eyes hiding in the brim's shadow. "I am too. Although you're making me look bad."

She wasn't sure if he was angry or poking fun at her. When the edge of his lips twitched upward, however, the tension in her body loosened. He was playing with her. A strange tingle fluttered in her stomach, and she couldn't deny the urge to play along.

She wrinkled her nose at him. "I doubt I could manage such a thing."

His eyes danced as his grin grew. "Is that so?"

A warmth spread into her cheeks, and she rubbed at one absently, dropping her eyes from his. Was she blushing?

"I doubt there's much that could make you look bad." She motioned toward his face, the deep blue eyes and the dark shadow of hair along his chin that made it look so sharp and strong. It wanted to be touched too. To be compared to the softer hair up top. When she realized she was staring at him, she cleared her throat, nearly falling into a coughing fit. "I mean, not you, but..." She looked away, a flutter of panic making her palms damp. "I guess I did make you look bad on the hunt."

There was a mischievous tilt to his eyebrow. A sly, almost shy smirk on his lips.

"I guess you did, Miss Tanner."

Heat itched up her neck and into her ears. A thrilling but uncomfortable feeling as thoughts of Papa found their way into her mind. What would he think of her if he could see her now? Talking and blushing in front of an outlaw.

She was supposed to be at tea that morning with Robert even. Not saying such silly things to a man she didn't know.

Robert's family were highly respected and a proper part of the community. What would they think of her if they knew?

A new icy fear crept into her.

What did they think of her now? Gone, disappeared. Bedding down in a camp full of men.

Good heavens. Her head reeled. Would Robert still want her when she got back to Emerald Falls?

Even though she was coming with a handsome dowry, would Robert still find her a suitable wife after sleeping in a tent outside surrounded by thieves and murderers?

The fact that Clay was a Van den Berg made her being alone with him so much worse.

The people of Emerald Falls would be horrified to know she was smiling and laughing with one of the gang members that had been terrorizing them.

She was sure the town cared little about what she did normally, but they would when she became Robert's wife. She'd finally be a part of the community, and that's what she wanted.

She stared up at Clay and found deep dark eyes staring back. A new wave of itchy warmth crept up her neck, and she looked away.

"You should get that thing back to Clara," she murmured, dropping her gaze to count the colored leaves on the ground.

"You're right." His boots crunched as he moved, and she risked a glance in his direction. His back was to her, and he stooped to lift the deer. "Clara wants this one for dinner. She'll need time to dress it. Let's go."

Sadie stood next to Clover, trying to avert her eyes as Clay hoisted the deer onto his shoulder. The stag had to be over a hundred pounds, and he slung the thing up onto the back of his horse like he did it every day.

No wonder he had such wide shoulders under that jacket. And a hard chest that peaked through the opening of his shirt beneath.

The blush in her face crept up to her ears, and she snapped her eyes away.

Clay Pearson was an outlaw. A thief. A murderer. He was no man to admire. She shouldn't even be talking civilly to him. He'd kidnapped her for Lord's sake!

She still couldn't help but look up at him when he approached her.

"Need a hand?" he asked.

Before she could answer, his hands were on her waist, and she gasped. Her body stiffened as he lifted her in the air and plopped her sidesaddle onto the mare.

She grabbed the saddle horn to keep herself upright, nearly kicking a boot into Clay's face to catch her balance. He blinked wide at her, resting a hand on the folded fabric of her knee.

"Are you okay?"

She grabbed at the dress ruffles and shook them, pressing them back into place on her leg and doing her best to ignore the crazy stirring within her at the touch of his hand. Then she adjusted her seat, picking up the reins.

"I'm fine. It's cold out here. Can we get back to the fire?"

Not that she needed any more heat touching her face or neck, but the longer she was out there with him, the more confused she was becoming.

He regarded her for a moment before turning to his horse and mounting up.

"Sure. We'll go confirm your letter went out last night. I'm sure you're eager to hear from your aunt."

He urged Georgene forward, and Sadie followed with less

enthusiasm. If they received a letter back from Aunt Hilda at all, she'd be shocked. If it said anything but "Bite me" she'd do a chicken dance in the middle of main street.

Aunt Hilda wasn't going to give the Van den Berg gang any money to get her back. She'd probably pay them to get rid of Sadie or change her name.

She clenched her jaw and cursed herself silently. She didn't have room to flub her escape plans a second time. Once the gang found out she was broke and her aunt hated her, she'd be in real danger. She was going to need to get away before that.

CHAPTER 7

"That is exactly what we needed," Clara said as Clay lowered the deer to the ground on the outskirts of camp. "I found some carrots and onions yesterday. We'll have an excellent stew tonight. Did you get enough to eat earlier?"

Sadie hovered behind them, absently running a hand up and down her arm. It took a moment before she realized the woman was speaking to her.

"I'm fine, thank you."

"There's some more bread from breakfast in my tent if you want it. I wouldn't mind taking a break before getting to work on this stag. Let's go."

Sadie glanced at Clay. She wasn't sure how free she was to go about as she pleased in camp. She was a prisoner, after all, but it didn't seem as if she was under lock and key. Clay'd left her and a horse alone in the woods while he hunted, for goodness' sake.

A lot of good that did, though. She'd royally stomped all over that escape plan.

"Clay," a man's voice boomed across the camp.

The three of them turned. Ace stood outside the flap of

his tent, neatly trimmed chin lifted in the air and eyes locked on them.

"Excuse me, ladies," Clay murmured. He paused after a couple steps, turning back with a finger in the air and a furrow in his brow as he glanced between the two.

"She's fine here, Clay," Clara cut in with a grin. "I'll put her to work."

His eyes moved to Sadie—the dark ones that drew her in so deep she feared she'd say something stupid again—and her breath caught in her chest. He regarded her silently for a breath, gaze roaming her face and neck, then he nodded.

"I'll be back."

Sadie watched him march off, and a cool shiver snaked its way up her spine. As much as she'd wanted to flee just an hour ago, she found herself wishing she could go with him now.

He was just the one she knew best there, she told herself. She was in a camp full of strangers. Of course she'd rather stay with Clay. For now. Until she could get away.

"Hunting again?" Clara snickered.

Sadie snapped to attention. "What's that?"

"You seemed to be on the prowl. Combing over the camp with your eyes. Looking for something delectable," Clara said, bouncing her chin in Clay's direction.

Sadie's cheeks flushed, and she fanned at the warm air crowding her neck. "I was doing nothing of the sort. I was curious as to what Ace wanted."

Clara lifted a shoulder with a grin. "Nothing wrong with having a look."

Even just looking had stirred odd and unwelcome feelings in her earlier that morning. It was not something to be played with. "I would say there was," she said. "I am engaged and do not wish to participate in such silly games."

The blonde shrugged again as she led the way to her tent.

"I'm not judging. I was just describing what I saw. Nothing to be ashamed of."

"That's right. Especially if nothing was happening."

A row over from the tent she'd stayed in the night before sat a cluster of four other lean-to dwellings. The nearest one was dressed with a ram's head hanging from the center post. A barrel and crate sat outside the white blanket tent flap. A sheet of paper and a pen sat on the crate, a make-shift table.

Clara disappeared inside the tent. Sadie stepped up to the corner of the structure and waited, gazing down at the paper. She'd expected words to be scrawled there, but instead found a sketch of a landscape. Rolling hills and trees. The detail was grand, and she leaned over for a better look.

"I don't blame you a bit," Clara said as she emerged from the tent, the butt end of a bread loaf in one hand and a canvas bag in the other. "Those Pearson boys are something to look at it."

Sadie frowned. "Tom looks at me like he might rip my throat out. There's nothing handsome about him." Although he did have the same strong build and chiseled jaw as Clay. She'd been too busy trying not to make eye contact with Tom that she'd barely noticed.

"It's a dark kind of handsome. Like Ace." She let out a low whistle as she handed over the bread. "That man has the best looking concentration face I've seen on this side of the Mississippi."

Sadie's nose wrinkled. "Concentration face?"

"Girl, wait until you see him hard at work." Clara shifted her feet to pop out a hip and fan at her neck. "I sit in on those boring progress meetings just to watch him read over his papers and point at the map."

She snickered, but Sadie scratched at the sun-kissed hair swirling loose behind her ear.

"But he's a bad man."

"Not to me. He gave me food and a place to sleep. I have a job here now, and I'm thankful."

Clara led the way back to the deer, and Sadie hurried to keep up.

"Why are you out here anyway? I thought all the women out here were—" She stopped, an uneasy feeling weighing on her stomach.

Clara paused as she reached inside the bag. "Painted ladies?"

Sadie flinched. Her voice barely squeaked above a whisper. "Maybe."

The edge of Clara's lip turned up. "It's ok. I thought that too. Before I joined them, that is." She pulled out a cluster of onions and carrots and stuffed them into Sadie's arms.

"Ace takes in those that need takin' in," she continued. "For whatever reason. I'd been traveling for three days when he and Tom ran across me down by the river. I don't think I'd have made it another day. I had no food, no horse, no protection." She shook her head as a subtle shudder rippled through her shoulders. "I thought I was going to die, but Ace brought me to camp, back when it was over back that way near St. Aspen. He gave me my own tent and made sure no one bothered me. I've been here ever since."

Sadie's stomach felt heavy. The very idea of being alone to defend for herself made her queasy. It was bad enough living with Papa so far from town her entire life, but if she had to do it without him? Beneath the stack of vegetables, she pressed a hand to her abdomen in an attempt to calm the writhing within.

Thank goodness she had Robert to go back to. She'd finally be a normal citizen of Emerald Falls.

Clara pulled two sheathed blades from her bag and placed one on the ground next to her. "Here. Cut those for me, will you?"

Sadie shifted the carrots and onions in her arms as she knelt in the grass. Clara got to work skinning the deer, and Sadie's nostrils flared as she turned a blind eye and set to work on the vegetables. She'd never liked the skinning part of her father's profession.

"Where were you going?" she asked, separating the onions on the canvas bag and picking up the knife.

"When I was lost?" Clara shook her head. "I was running from the law."

Sadie stopped and stared. Clara continued without looking up.

"I told him I wasn't going to take it anymore. I guess he didn't believe me."

"Who?"

"My husband."

Clara wiped her hands on a rag and stood to strip the deer. Sadie watched her with a dumb slack in her jaw.

"He was a miserable man. Nothing made him happy. Not me. Not his mama. It wasn't long before the whiskey didn't make him happy either. When he got lost in that rage, he was like a bull. Any movement would set him off. It was best just to stay out of his way. Except I wanted to help." Clara rolled her eyes and yanked harder on the deer hide. "Stupid me, always trying to find a way to make it better. I can't tell you how many times he hit me, but it only took a couple weeks before I told him. I said, Lloyd, if you touch me again I'm going to come after you with that repeater your father gave you. He just didn't believe me."

She shrugged and rolled the half-skinned deer over. "I don't lie. He should have listened."

Sadie's mouth had turned to cotton. Clara had seemed so normal and sweet. She'd even been thankful Clara was there at the camp to keep her company. And safe. She'd felt much more at ease with Clara around. At least she had before she knew the truth.

"You—you killed him?"

Clara stood and looked down at Sadie, hands resting on her hips with her skinning knife turned out away from her back. "I sure did. That bastard won't hurt me ever again."

Sadie's nostrils flared, and she swallowed back a knot of nerves and the threat of a heave. She'd never met a murderous woman before. Or at least one that freely admitted to it. She was sure all the men she'd come in contact with in camp had killed people. They were outlaws, after all.

Clara had seemed different. Normal.

She'd been so blind.

Clara dropped her knife and wiped her hands as she knelt next to her. Her brow creased, and she set a hand on Sadie's shoulder. Sadie fought the urge to shudder and lean away.

"He broke my arm, Sadie. Once he pummeled my face until I couldn't see for two days. The daily bruises and the fear. He was going to kill me. The worst part was he was the one that was supposed to be protecting me. Who was going to protect me from him? No one, that's who. So I did."

Her fingers flexed on Sadie's shoulder. Sadie stared at the blonde as she let the words sink in. She'd known a battered woman in Emerald Falls. She was a sad sight for years. Quiet and meek. She came running every time her husband barked her name. They all knew what was going on, but no one ever reacted. It was a sad ordeal. She supposed that woman should have been more like Clara.

"I wouldn't let him ruin me," Clara murmured. "But you don't have to be afraid of me, Sadie. I won't hurt you."

Despite the small inklings of fear still tickling around the edge of her conscience, Sadie smiled. "I'm glad. I like being around you."

Clara's face brightened. "And I you. Let's get this dinner going."

She went back to the deer, and Sadie concentrated on the onions again. She glanced Clara's way a time or two, watching her skill with the knife, but her worries had dissipated.

Once the hide was free, Clara rolled it and set it aside.

"I can help with that later if you'd like," Sadie offered.

"You can tan hides?"

Sadie gave an exasperated eye-roll with a smile. "I've probably tanned a few hundred."

Clara blinked at her, eyebrows set high. "Really?"

"Yes. My father sold skins. He did the hunting and skinning. I cured the hides."

"Brilliant. The only skill my father taught me was to stick up for myself. It came in handy, since he married me off to a real jerk."

Sadie winced. "That's an ironic twist."

"Don't I know it. I don't trust any daddy arranged marriage."

Sadie paused, knife halfway through her third onion. She opened her mouth to reply but thought better of it. Clara must have noticed.

"I'm sorry. Is yours an arranged marriage?"

"Well, sort of. The Murphys are a big name in Emerald Falls. I'm lucky I was chosen. They push cattle across five thousand acres."

Clara nodded with wide eyes. "Impressive. Your fiancé—what did you say his name was? Robert? He owns it?"

"His father does. He's the oldest of three boys."

"Do you like him?"

Sadie stiffened at the comment. "Of course I do. We're to be married."

Clara snorted as she set aside two cuts of meat. "I'm not sure that really answers the question. I assume you don't love him, but do you even like him? He's not one of those spoiled ranchers, is he?"

Sadie scoffed. "Of course not. He's very respectable. He knows how to treat a lady properly. I'll certainly be moving up in the world once I join that family. Thank goodness for that, since I've been unceremoniously deprived of my father." She didn't expect the hitch in her breath at the mention of Papa. Rather than give in to the ache in her chest, she bit the inside of her cheek and forced the emotions back down.

Clara stopped working, and one of her eyebrows quirked up. "Does he know you can handle a rifle?"

Sadie brushed aside leftover onion skins with a snappy wrist. "As a matter of fact, he does. He's seen me use one. He didn't care for it, but he saw it. He should thank heavens I can too!"

Clara's eyes flashed in amusement. "Do tell. Did you shoot someone?"

Sadie paused mid-flick of vegetable parts. She hadn't meant to say that out loud. The last thing she wanted was to admit that her betrothed had rolled over in the face of danger. It was less than becoming of a man. No one had seen it but her, and as his future wife, she should keep the details to herself.

Clara's eyes bored into her. She was like raccoons in winter, greedy and ready to gobble up any scraps thrown out into the snow.

Sadie couldn't find it in herself to lie outright. She'd already said it. It was best just to get it over with.

"I didn't shoot a person, no."

"What was it? Were you being attacked?"

Sadie pinched the bridge of her nose with a soft sigh.

Drat. She'd stepped in it. She lowered her hand and went back to cutting carrots like the story was most uninteresting.

"We were attacked by a wolf on the edge of town. I don't know what he was doing so close to the people, but he seemed off. Like he was hurt or sick. He was so angry." She cleared her throat as she chopped. "I had a gun on the wagon, but Robert tried to stop me from getting it. Weapons were unbecoming for a lady, he'd said. But I grabbed it anyway. Thankfully. Because that wolf ran for Robert like he was going to rip him to shreds." She shuddered. "It was a clean shot, dropped the beast. I don't know if Robert was more relieved or horrified that I'd saved him. He's never made mention of the incident again, to me or anyone else."

"I wouldn't either," Clara smirked. "If he was that upset about you just touching a rifle, what's he going to say when you get back home? Unchaperoned and out shooting deer?"

Sadie grimaced. It was what she kept pushing from her mind. She didn't want to think about his reaction.

"I suppose he'll be shocked. Angry. His mother even more so."

"She a bad one?"

"She's rather odd."

Clara perked an eyebrow. "Odd?"

"Uptight. She bosses her sons around a good bit. The only one that talks over her is Mr. Murphy. He doesn't talk much, but when he does, she listens. I wish she'd talk less most of the time."

Clara cackled. "I've known women like that. Can't say I care for them much."

Sadie shook her head. "Not when they're so bossy. It's a wonder Robert can do anything on his own. She's always right there over his shoulder. If only she were more like Lilah, Robert's sister. She barely speaks. It's so quiet and peaceful."

"At least you'll have someone around that won't drive you nuts."

Sadie pressed her lips together as a fog of unease settled over her, but she nodded. One person in her new family that wasn't frightening or ridiculous. Except Lilah was too quiet and horribly dull. Maybe there would be no one she could relate to there.

"You sound like you at least like Robert though. That's good. Although I'd say he's not my cup of tea. Not like the good looking fellow you shot this deer for. I'm sure he'd let you protect him any time."

Sadie's shoulders squared, and an odd feeling raced through her stomach. "I'm sure he wouldn't."

"You could ask him. He's headed this way."

CHAPTER 8

A warm flush stretched up Sadie's neck and into her ears as she looked over her shoulder. Clay's solid form was weaving through the tents in their direction. The late morning sun gleaned off his soft honey-colored hair. His thumbs were tucked into the edges of his belt, and his expression was set in what she'd come to realize was his resting face. Stoic, a small crease in the brow, like he was both thinking of something serious and ready for a challenge. The guise looked good on him.

As he neared, Sadie ducked down low and went back to work prepping vegetables.

"That was a good shot on the deer," Clara said, bent over her work and giving a short glance to Clay's boots as he stopped next to her. "Are you sure Sadie made it?"

A deep grunt that sounded almost like a chuckle escaped him. "I was surprised too."

"Good to know a girl that can shoot like that, huh?"

Sadie looked up at Clara, who wore a titillating grin.

"Not all men are afraid of women with guns," Clara continued. "I mean, my husband should have been, but I know you're secure enough to handle it, right, Clay? Unlike Sadie's fiancé. It makes him sick."

"Fiancé?" Clay rumbled.

Sadie wasn't sure if it was the small flash in his hard blue eyes or the way Clara grinned stupidly at his reaction, but Sadie felt her stomach turn over. If she'd been holding anything less lethal than a knife, she'd have chunked it at Clara. She wasn't even sure why, as she'd only told the truth, but the way Clay's body tightened at the word made Sadie's cheeks burn hot.

Then his eyes were on her, and the blood drained from her face. They captured her. Both lifted her off the ground to float among the clouds and crushed her down into the grass with the soft confused crease in his brow.

"You're engaged?"

Sadie swallowed.

Yes. She was. To a good man living within the law of society. In a town she wanted to be a part of. His family was well known and loved all along the Absaroka plains. She had a chance to be a part of that, and it was everything she wanted.

So why was it so hard to answer Clay?

Her fingers trembled, and she tucked her knife into its sheath. Something ripped. She gasped and looked down.

The knife had missed the sheath and pierced through the front ruffles of her dress. Its sharp edge had sliced through the top layers, nearly reaching her leg. She dropped the knife on the ground and stood, grabbing at the gaping hole.

Clara leapt to her rescue, blocking Clay's view of Sadie's skirts. Sadie managed to bunch the dress enough to hide the hole, but her blush had returned tenfold.

Clay cleared his throat, averting his eyes.

"Did I hear someone say this one is engaged?" Tom asked as he clapped a hand on Clay's shoulder and came around from behind him.

Sadie gaped at them, shuffling around to hide her front from the men. What horrible timing. And awful luck.

"Yes," Clay murmured. "She has a fiancé back home."

Tom looked at Sadie with an interested perk in his eyebrow. He sized her up, and she fought the shudder bunching in her shoulders. Then he looked pointedly at his brother.

Clay regarded him silently. His jaw flexed. When his eyes turned on her, they were dull, uninterested. They hit her in the chest even before his words.

"Think he'd pay more for you than your aunt?"

Sadie's insides rolled, a cloud swelling in her head like she'd been kicked in the crown. It was the first time Clay'd mentioned the money since she'd arrived, and it cut deep.

"Piss off, Pearsons," Clara growled. "She's not a horse at auction."

She wrapped an arm around Sadie's waist and led her back into the campsite.

"She's not a doll for you to play with either," Tom barked. "She's going to bring us in a good pile of money. We need it. You know that. You ain't going to ruin this one for us."

Clara narrowed her eyes over her shoulder, then looked to Clay. "Bring that meat in for me. It'll spoil out here."

"I've got it, Miss Clara."

His voice was softer, less stern, but Sadie didn't look back to check his expression. Instead, she let Clara shuttle her off toward her tent.

Sadie hovered just inside the flap, her head still reeling from Clay's question. Would Robert pay more money for her than Aunt Hilda? Of course he would, if he had more. His family was well off, but they also had a working cattle operation. He probably didn't have the kind of extra cash the Van den Bergs wanted. Definitely not as much as Aunt Hilda.

He'd give it away faster than that witch. Or at least she hoped he would.

Neither option was a reliable one. She'd need to keep up her wealthy aunt facade until she could devise a plan to escape, before they found out the truth.

But she couldn't make her brain focus. No matter how many times she blinked, she couldn't clear the cold blue eyes from her head.

She'd thought Clay wasn't as bad as the others. He was nothing like she'd imagined an outlaw. He was kind and helpful. Flirty and handsome. He had his hard edges, but something about him drew her in and made her want to learn more.

Then he'd spouted off that horrible question, and her image of him popped like a bubble.

Her teeth clenched. She felt like a fool. Why on earth had her mind wandered, thinking Clay was a decent man? Why did that bright look in his eyes stir her stomach like the first leap off of Horner Cliff into the frigid water below? Just like the lake in early spring, his eyes had turned cold and biting.

She shivered.

"Sometimes these men are just ridiculous," Clara said as she pulled Sadie further into her tent. "Always obsessed with money. Not that we don't need it. I mean, there's a lot of people to care for here, and we generally don't have much money."

Sadie hmphed in response.

"But that's no excuse. I hate how Tom treats Clay."

Sadie frowned. "Tom?"

Clara popped open a small chest at the foot of her bed and rifled through the contents. "Don't tell me you didn't notice that change. Tom orders Clay around like a dog."

Sadie'd been so shocked by Clay's words that she hadn't

given their reason any thought. They had been too swift and cold.

"He doesn't seem like an idiot. Can't he think for himself?"

Clara scoffed as she pulled some garments from the chest. "Of course he can, but that's not how these guys are around here. There's a hierarchy."

"Outlaw gangs have hierarchies?"

An amused smirk crossed Clara's face as she handed Sadie a pair of trousers. "Sure they do. Here. These might not be what you're used to, but they'll make do while you get your dress fixed."

Sadie unfolded the pants and held them up. Brown cotton that didn't look too big. "Thank you. I've never heard the politics of a gang. I thought they were just rowdy crowds of thieves and murderers."

Clara gave a small wince. "It's not that cut and dry. Some gangs are pretty bad. A few are mostly non-violent. It's just a group of people, after all."

Sadie stared at the blonde with a sour face. She wasn't sure which was a harder pill to swallow, learning that the outlaw gang that'd been terrorizing Emerald Falls was made up of much more normal people than she'd ever imagined, or admitting that she was constantly misjudging them.

"Let me help you with that," Clara said, slinging an extra shirt over her shoulder and assisting with Sadie's dress laces. "I'm sure you usually have someone to help you with this."

"Help me? Of course not. I dress myself."

"Oh, I thought maybe…"

"We didn't have help. We barely had enough money to take care of ourselves."

Clara's voice dropped and scratched in her throat. "My apologies. I just saw—you have a beautiful dress."

"Thank you. It was my mother's. We were traveling for a special occasion."

Truth told, she more often wore trousers like Clara's. It was easier to work with the animals and help Papa with the tanning in pants. She had simpler dresses she went to town and met Robert in.

Clara worked silently until the dress fell limp and handed the shirt over before turning away. Sadie slipped out of the dress and stepped into her borrowed clothes.

In the corner of the tent, Clara cracked a grin as she busied herself with stacking a few books near her sleeping pallet.

"I knew he liked you."

Sadie paused with the long-sleeved white shirt pulled halfway over her head. "What?"

"Clay. You got him all flustered back there."

Sadie frowned, yanking the shirt down in place. It was a little large, but it would work just fine until she had more clothes. "Me? You were the one spouting off about Robert and making those men salivate over more money. How silly."

Clara coughed out a laugh, looking back with a grin so wide it made her cheek dimple. "Are you telling me you didn't see Clay's heart break when I told him you were engaged?"

Sadie had seen him stiffen up, and she'd heard the way his voice wavered when he spoke. "He was only excited about the money. I revealed another source of cash they could get their grubby hands on. I'll be more careful next time."

Clara popped a hip out and stuck a hand to it. "You need to get your eyes checked if that's what you think. I took the wind right out of that boy's sails telling him that."

"That wasn't very nice of you," Sadie murmured, letting the words sink in a little deeper. Had Clay's heart really broken right in front of her? Had that beautiful blue spark in his eye gone out because he'd learned the truth?

"I just wanted to see where his heart was," Clara said, picking up Sadie's dress and draping it across the bottom of her pallet. "I wasn't expecting that much of a reaction though. At least, now we know."

Amusement had crept back into Clara's smile. She was having fun with the game. Sadie didn't know what to think of it. A part of her wanted to latch onto the notion. Something about the idea that Clay's heart could feel for her made her pulse flicker. But then he'd turned those dead eyes on her. The same sharp, dark eyes as his brother. No one that looked at her like that could possibly have feelings for her.

"Last night he called me a city girl, with the worst scowl I've ever seen on a man. I don't think he has any interest in me."

Clara's eyebrows perked. "Ah, yes. Clay's bane." She let out a hoot of laughter. "That boy poor worked so hard to fit in with those city girls. It about broke him apart."

Sadie tucked a tail of the long shirt into her pants. "He tried to fit in with them?" The very idea of the rustic outlaw trying to get by in the city was too much for her to imagine.

"Sure. You do stupid things when you're in love, I guess."

Sadie's heart skipped a beat, and her mouth went dry. "He was in love with a city girl?"

Clara crossed her arms over her chest with a lighthearted shrug. "I doubt it. You think you are at the time though, you know? I loved my husband once upon a time." She let out a low whistle. "But Clay, he belongs to this life. He's not made to wear nice suits and work in a factory, but he tried it. For about a week."

"What happened?"

"He went off to St. Aspen with some girl. Pretty thing. Dressed really nice. She didn't know the first thing about life outside the city though. I guess he thought she was worth the lifestyle change, but it wasn't for him. All the dinner parties and politics. He said so many of them were false. Fake smiles, fake words. It was impossible to tell what people actually wanted. And if you did want something, you didn't earn it. You paid for it."

"I suppose that does sound more like the city life."

Clara nodded. "You can't make yourself fit into a puzzle you don't belong in though. The men and women there were soft, and no one could take care of themselves. I suppose that's what got Clay in the end. Changing everything he knew was hard enough, but the girl was too weak to handle him. She needed someone to wait on her, dress her, and never did anything to help herself. I suppose that's why he was so impressed with you shooting that deer." Clara's eyebrow arched, and she grinned mischievously.

"Dream all you want," Sadie said with a shrug. "I'm just looking forward to getting out of here and starting my life with Robert."

It was a phrase that'd rolled around in her head for ages. She'd looked forward to escaping her life with Papa in the cabin in the woods. The thought of leaving him had often weighed on her, but she was excited to be a real part of a community. Robert was her ticket to that.

Whatever she had to do to make that happen, she would. Even if it meant burying all Clara's giggly gossip and Clay's beautiful eyes away forever.

CHAPTER 9

Later that afternoon, Sadie stood at the edge of the campfire, stirring the contents of a large black pot. The simmering of venison and fresh vegetables made her mouth water. Grief had still been heavy in her stomach that morning, and she'd skipped breakfast. After a hard day's work following, it felt as if it had been days since she'd last eaten.

"That smells mighty nice," a man said as he came around the fire behind her.

Sadie moved aside to let him come into the community space. He stepped around one of the many barrels and seats arranged around the fire pit and settled himself in.

He wore simple trousers and a thermal shirt. His face split into a grin that reached his eyes, and he popped the white hat on his head up with a finger. She recognized that hat. It was one of the men who'd been watching her the night before outside of Ace's tent.

"I'm starving," he said. "I hope that's ready."

"It is," she said. Some of the nerves that had bunched inside her when he appeared, a random gang member she'd only seen once from across the camp, eased at the sight of his bright smile.

"Can I get two of those bowls?" he asked, nodding to the stack Clara had dropped off moments before.

Sadie retrieved two of the utensils and held them out for the stranger. He pointed around her at the pot.

"And some of that stew?"

Sadie frowned back at the pot. She wasn't a food server any more than she was a seamstress, which is why she still stood in Clara's borrowed clothes.

"Um, sure."

Clara stepped up next to her and picked up two more bowls. "Go ahead and scoop them some. It's better if we do it rather than let those dirty boys stick their hands in the pot." She winked as she spooned out some stew.

Sadie nodded as she did the same. "I used to cook for my father every day. It'll be strange not doing that anymore."

"Don't worry. You'll have a new husband to cook for."

"If he'll still have me."

Clara passed a bowl to another fellow that approach, skin as black as coal, and grinned. "Honey, you're not missing out on a damn thing. I cooked for my husband for five years before I left. I swore I'd never do it again, but then I got here. No one demands I do it, but they appreciate it. It feels different."

It must because she smiled as she handed out food. One by one. Tom, Ace, and the two rascals Tom had been cutting up with that morning sat at one end of the fire. A tall woman with long ringlets of red hair stepped into the circle and sat beside the man with the white hat. She looped her arm through his and pressed her cheek into his shoulder. He practically melted into her.

"Here we go," Sadie said as she handed him the bowls.

"Thank you," he took both, passing one to the woman at his side.

She cupped the bowl in both hands but made no movement to sit up and eat. She seemed content nestled there, her body contoured to his and her nose rubbing against the shirt on his shoulder. Was she smelling him? Sadie averted her eyes for a moment, wondering if she was intruding in an intimate moment, but she couldn't keep them away for long.

The way his arm slid around her back and pulled her in closer, hand lingering on her waist, made a shiver tickle through her spine. They looked so comfortable and relaxed. Safe and content. That woman must have nothing to fear tucked into him like that.

When the man's eyes caught Sadie's, she cleared her throat and went back to stirring the pot.

"So you're the Miss Tanner I've heard the boys talking about?"

A bashful flutter tickled her cheeks. "I am."

"I guess these are weird circumstances, but you seem like a mighty fine lady. It's nice to meet you. Name's Mason Kent."

The man set his bowl on his knees and stretched out a hand. Sadie stared at it a moment as if it might bite her before placing her fingers in his.

"Nice to meet you, Mr. Kent."

"Oh, please. Call me Mason. This is Bridget."

The woman next to him smiled around a mouthful of stew and lifted her bowl. "Pleasure to meet you. This is delicious."

"Well, that was Clara," Sadie said, jerking a thumb over her shoulder.

"I heard you were bringing in some money," Mason interrupted. "They got a ransom on you or are you a—"

Clara cut in, slipping an arm around Sadie's shoulders.

"She's visiting for a few days and making a charitable donation." She lifted a brow with pursed lips at Mason. "What are you doing asking questions anyway? You know what a girl held against her will looks like."

Sadie saw the subtle turn of Clara's head in Bridget's direction and the way the red-headed woman busied herself in her stew. The bright demeanor on Mason's face sagged a bit before he nodded.

"Right. Sorry. Glad to have you with us, Miss Tanner."

"It's Sadie," she offered.

The couple fell into their dinner silently. Clara gave Sadie a strong pat on the shoulder.

"We're not big believers in the ransoming thing around here," the blonde said. "Holding others against their will. Bridget there was a captive when we met her. Lucky for her Mason has a weak heart and rescued her."

The sparkle in Mason's eyes returned, and he bumped his shoulder lightly into his companion. "It didn't take much to win me over, I admit. Ain't she beautiful?"

Bridget's cheeks turned pink, and she smiled up at him. The two lovebirds made eyes at each other, and Sadie shifted to turn her back on them, an embarrassed smile on her face.

"They're like puppies," she whispered.

"You have no idea," Clara snickered. "Regular Romeo and Juliet there."

Sadie blinked. "You've read Romeo and Juliet?"

"Sweetie, just 'cause I live in the woods doesn't mean I never went to school."

Sadie bit into her lower lip. "Well, I didn't mean…"

"It's okay, but it's true. Romeo and Juliet right there. It came with the feuding and the whole lot. Thankfully most everything is back to normal, and their ending turned out much better than Shakespeare's."

Sadie stole a peek at the couple just in time to see Mason

run his fingers through the long fiery locks while Bridget finished her stew. It was adorable.

"What was the feud about?" she whispered back to Clara.

"She'd been living with—"

Clara's words were cut off by the sound of approaching hooves. Everyone went silent, and Sadie looked around. The crew was frozen, listening. It was then she realized what a large group had gathered around the fire. At least ten were posed with bowls in hand.

Except for Clay.

Her heart fumbled through a beat, wondering where he'd gone off to. She'd only just begun to wonder if the gang was expecting someone dangerous and if Clay was alright when he appeared through the trees at the edge of the tents. A shovel dragged the ground behind him before he dropped it outside one of the dwellings.

The dull hum of conversation started up again. The white-bearded fellow sitting next to Ace laughed above the others.

"Where the hell you been? Been digging for gold, boy?"

Clay's eyes were cold when he looked at him. "Unfortunately not." Then his gaze jumped to Sadie, and she started. His eyes shifted, opening and softening. "I had to bury a body."

Her breath caught, and her chest constricted as the realization hit her instantly.

He'd buried her father.

She dropped the ladle into the pot and strode to the side of the circle, high stepping over a square hay bale turned into a seat. Clay stood just beyond the perimeter, dusty hands shoved into his pockets. She drove herself forward without a second thought and wrapped her arms around his neck, pressing her burst of tears into his shoulder.

"Thank you," she choked.

He stumbled a step back, but his hands moved around her shoulders to embrace her in return. His body was stiff, but his arms were warm. After a silent moment, he patted her back.

"You're welcome."

Feeling suddenly self-conscious, she leaned away, wiping at her wet cheeks with her wrist.

"I'm sorry. I just—"

The edge of Clay's mouth turned up, and he rubbed at her back with a hand that still remained. "It's alright, Miss Tanner."

Clara cleared her throat behind them. "Clay, you hungry?"

He looked up over Sadie's head. "I'm starving."

"Come get some of this food then. Hurry it up. I can't hold off the piglets all night."

Clay gave Sadie's arm a final pat and stepped around her. At first, she felt a chill, standing away from the fire without his body to block the wind. Then his voice was near her ear.

"Have you eaten?"

She looked over her shoulder and found his face so close to her that a flush rose up in her chest and neck. Those big blue eyes looked deeper than ever, and they beckoned her.

"Not yet."

"Better get you some." He stepped over the hay bale and into the fire circle, then offered her a hand. "It really might disappear before the night's out."

"Thank you." She put her hand in his and let him help her over the hay. On the other side, he eased her down to sit on the hay. She did.

"He's right," Clara said, handing a bowl off to Clay. "Food goes fast around here."

He gave the stew to Sadie, who nodded her thanks. When he had another, he sat next to her. At first, it was hard to concentrate on her dinner with his hip brushing against hers, but he was quite preoccupied with eating, and it smelled so good. She dug in.

Mason and Bridget struck up a conversation with Clara. She sat next to them while the rest of the gang finished off their food.

After a moment of quiet eating, a heavyset fellow nearby placed his bowl aside and drew out a handgun. Sadie's muscles clenched, and she sat a little taller, ready to run if need be. Clay shifted next to her and rested a hand on her knee. Despite the adrenaline coursing through her veins, her body relaxed.

"I ain't been able to clear this thing out since I dropped it in that mud hole," the gun wielder said. "What am I gone do with it?"

Clay nodded his chin in his direction. "I can take a look at that in the morning, Otis. I've cleaned mud out of one of mine before."

"My thanks," the man said, stretching across the circle to hand his revolver over.

Clay reached across Sadie to take the gun. His arm brushed her shoulder, but it wasn't as weird and unwelcome as she expected. She watched silently as he checked that the revolving cylinder was empty and slid the gun into the pocket on his opposite hip.

Otis laughed aloud. "That girl look like she's never seen a gun before. Don't worry, sweetie. It ain't loaded."

Sadie narrowed her eyes a fraction, a sassy perk in the corner of her mouth. "A gun is only dangerous in the wrong hands."

"That's right. So don't be touching—"

"She shot that deer in your dinner," Clay offered simply, nodding his head at Otis's empty bowl.

The men exchanged a look, then Otis returned his utensils to the center of the circle and moved off into the encroaching darkness beyond the fire.

A deep chuckle rumbled in Clay's chest, and he bumped her lightly in the shoulder.

Sadie looked up at him with a soft sigh. "Thank you. I know I'm just a—what was it you called me? A city girl?—but I can hold my own."

"I believe you can, but that's good. Can't say I expected you to be shooting guns. Or to be dressed in trousers when I came back." His eyes roamed down her legs, and Sadie's cheeks burned. "Survivors learn to make do with their situations, and I believe that's what you are. A survivor."

Her chest swelled, and she smiled. She'd never been called a survivor before, but she liked the sound of it. If she'd survived that long in a band of murdering thieves, she could survive anything it seemed like.

Except the longer she stayed, the more she realized the Van den Berg gang wasn't just made up of killers and train robbers. They were people, some of them more civilized than some townspeople she knew.

Clay set his bowl aside and leaned back, resting his hands on the back of their hay bale. As he did so, his shoulder brushed hers again, but this time it didn't move away. It pressed into her, solid and warm. Despite any stray feelings of fear or animosity circling inside her, she liked the way it felt. She leaned into his shoulder as well, staring into the fire in front of them.

Many of the others dropped their bowls off and wandered away. Ginny and Jack started up a duet, guitar and vocals, of a song Sadie had known since she was a child. She hummed along. They made it through two songs before Jack started fumbling through his chords and laughing. He wasn't quite as drunk as the night before, but he was well on his way. Sadie grinned as the two musicians cackled at one another in their attempt to play.

Then her eyes crossed the fire and found Clara staring at her. The woman's head gave a curious tilt as she looked between Sadie and Clay. Sadie peeked up at Clay, who also wore a grin as he stared at Jack making a fool of himself. Then she lowered her eyes to his shoulder. Big, safe, and not who she should be leaning on.

She reached her arms out in front of her in an exaggerated stretch, rolling her shoulders, and, as casually as she could manage, leaning off of Clay.

Her arm was cold, and she couldn't deny the disappointment settling in her stomach. Her wedding date was in a few months. She was growing less and less sure how Robert would receive her when she returned, but getting cozy around the fire with Clay certainly wouldn't improve her situation.

Sadie cut her eyes across the fire again, fighting the frustration building in her muscles, but Clara was laughing with Ginny. With an irritated breath, Sadie stood and excused herself. Suddenly being alone on her pallet on the hard ground seemed better than around the warm fire with friendly company.

CHAPTER 10

Sadie felt better that morning than she had the last. Her father's death was heavy on her soul still, but she was much more at peace knowing he'd been given a burial rather than left on the plains for the bears. Then her thoughts had wandered to Clay.

He'd ridden back to take care of Papa, even after Tom's dirty refusal. Clara had made Clay sound like such a pawn. That he only followed orders.

But he'd broken them. To help her.

A small smile crossed Sadie's face as she plucked a small orange fruit from a basket next to the fire pit. The early morning sun was still dim, and the camp was empty. The coyote yips had died down not long before, and the songbirds were just starting to rouse themselves.

Sadie wanted to talk to Clara about what had happened the night before. Something about the look the blonde had given her made her feel like a scolded child, caught with her fingers in the sweet stash. She'd just been eating with Clay. It was the least she could do after what he'd done for her. She may have bumped his shoulder a few times, but it had been nothing as well.

Hadn't it?

Sadie poked at the orange peel lightly as she recalled the evening. It wasn't as if she'd never brushed shoulders with a man before. It happened in crowded spaces. But it wasn't normally so warm and inviting as Clay's. She may have leaned into it a little too much, for a little too long. He hadn't objected.

Her lips twitched in the smallest of smiles.

Approaching footsteps drew her attention, and she straightened.

"You're up early." Clay's deep drawl reached her even before she saw the top of his hat over the nearest tent.

When he came around the edge of it, the sun lit up the sly grin on his face. Sadie's insides did a somersault.

"I suppose I had a better night's sleep," she murmured, eyes transfixed on his mouth.

The upper half of his face was hidden in the shadow of his hat, but as he got closer, she found his handsome eyes fixed on her.

"I'm glad to hear it. I hope it's not too cold in there for you."

"Your fire helps." She swallowed a lump in her throat. "The one you've kept going outside my tent, I mean."

He stopped outside the circle of seats around the fire pit, regarding her with a curious tilt of his hat. "How do you know it's been me keeping that fire up? I'm a busy man."

She bit into the inside of her lip, swayed by the soft growl in his voice. She'd seen him tend to the fire a few times, once in the middle of the night. Instead of calling him out, she just lifted a shoulder. "Just an assumption, I suppose."

His lips pursed slightly as the last fraction of his mouth quirked up. They stared at one another in silence, and his eyes moved down her form and back up slowly. Heat blossomed in her cheeks as she recalled her outfit. She probably looked like a ragged boy dressed in trousers and an oversized shirt. She had tucked the shirt in and pinned it to a better size, but it was far from anything she wanted to be seen in. It wasn't as if she were in the woods working with Papa.

Then his eyes were on hers again, both clouded and sharp in a manner she couldn't describe. She was on the verge of asking if anything was the matter when he spoke.

"I was just going to take Georgene down to the river for an early drink. It's pretty down there in the morning. Would you like to accompany me?"

It hadn't been at all what she expected. She stared at him, trying to keep her eyes from widening too much.

He wanted her to go off alone with him.

They'd done the same the day before on their hunt, but it'd been different. She'd been his prisoner, and she'd been thankful she wasn't left alone at camp with all the strange men. This proposal felt different. She had a choice.

He dropped a hand from his belt and held it out in her direction. Her heart felt strangled in indecision as she stared at it. She knew better than to go off with men on her own. It wasn't becoming of a lady. It was doubly damning while she was engaged. But with every hour she lived among the Van den Bergs, the more she doubted Robert would accept her back. He would cut her off and cast her out.

It was such a horrible fate that she'd been constantly stuffing it down deep inside. It was better not to focus on it.

So she didn't. She did what she knew she would do from the moment Clay moved his hand toward her.

She took it.

He led her through the camp and underneath the first overhanging tree branches of the forest at the edge of the clearing. Two brown horses looked up as they eased their way into the animals' space. A small herd of horses was crowded around a single wooden trough there in the shadow of the trees. Most of them were dozing with their heads lowered. A few watched as the people approached.

Georgene stood near the center of the group. She swished her tail, a unique blend of black and white strands, when Clay rested his free hand on her rump and gave her a pat.

"Good morning, girl," he said.

The horse blew out a whuffling breath.

Clay backed Georgene out of the herd and nodded his head to the gray mare Sadie'd ridden before.

"Did you like that Clover horse?"

"She was a smooth ride."

"Good. We'll take her again."

The horses were saddled and ready to move. Clay led Sadie to Clover's side and helped her up. Then he hopped into Georgene's saddle, and they set off down a path through the woods.

The cool morning air was warming, and a few short bursts of bird songs drifted down from the trees. Leaves rustled, and a rabbit sprang across their path. Clover snorted but continued on without a fuss.

The silence was calming. Even though Sadie was curious what had prompted Clay to ask her to join him, she was enjoying the peace and quiet out of camp with him.

It was a wonder to watch him riding along, moving as one with Georgene. He barely moved a hand or a foot, and she followed along. He held a soft rein and didn't pull on her bit. He also scratched fingers along her neck and shoulder every so often.

Watching him made Sadie smile.

"Georgene must be a special horse," she said.

Clay gave the horse another soft pat. "She is that. Raised her up from a baby. Mason picked up her mama from an abandoned farm. He didn't even realize she had a foal when he got there, but the horse was a good one, so he brought them both back. His girl wanted the baby, but she didn't know a darn thing about animals. So I got it."

Sadie tilted her head as they moved down the gradual slope to the river's edge. "He had another girl?"

Clay's brow creased. "Oh yeah. He was gonna marry that woman, he said. He was really torn up after she passed. For a long while. I thought he was going to leave us. But that Bridget." Clay's creases turned into a smile. "She fixed it up right."

The soft edges in Clay's face drew a smile to Sadie's mouth as well, and she lowered her head to keep from staring.

"I'm glad he's doing better," she said. "He seems like a nice person."

"He is."

The horses' hooves crunched into the pebbles and sand along the river bank. Georgene stepped into the first few inches of water and lowered her head to drink. Clay loosened her reins and let her relax. Sadie did the same as Clover followed suit.

"I've never had a horse I trusted as much as this ol' girl though," he continued. "She's been with me for years."

Sadie had heard a few cowboys speak of their horses in such a manner, but she'd never seen a pair together.

"It's sweet you care for her so much," she said, then felt silly for saying so. She couldn't quite comprehend the relationship.

Despite staring so intently at the water, she could feel Clay's eyes on her. After a moment she couldn't help but look up. Those hypnotic eyes were locked on her.

"I'm thankful she cares for me," he said, his voice low. "Even the best-trained horse can buck you off if he isn't up for doing what he's asked. Having a horse that will risk its neck for you and never blink an eye at braving danger to save your life. Now that's a jewel. I can't tell you how many times Georgene's saved my life."

Sadie stared at him, moved by his words. She'd never known a horse did so much to keep its rider safe. The good ones at least. Clay was clearly grateful.

As was she.

She looked at the smooth buckskin with a renewed sense of awe. The mare'd brought Clay far enough to meet her at least.

"She does sound truly special."

His eye twinkled as he looked up at her. "She is. I'm thankful Mason had a good head on his shoulders when he made the decision who should take Georgene."

A lump of nerves formed in Sadie's throat at the words. Maybe it was Clay's devotion in his relationship with the horse, or the way the morning reflections on the river danced in his eyes, or the tantalizing tilt at the edge of his lips when he looked at her, but she found herself bubbling over with a rush of feelings. They started deep in her stomach, and words leapt from her mouth before she had a moment to stop them.

"Good thing he has good judgment. Papa arranged my marriage without even consulting me."

As soon as the statement was out, she looked away, horrified that she'd spoken such a thing, but not before she'd seen his eyebrows pop, a silent engagement of intrigue.

It was only part truth after all. She'd been eager to find a husband. It was the only way that girls like her moved up and out of living in a cabin in the woods. She hadn't been a part of the process of securing Robert as her selection, but she hadn't disagreed. She'd heard Papa discussing matters of her dowry with Mr. Murphy, but she'd never inquired into the details. They didn't matter. She'd be leaving.

Now that future was a tangled mess. Papa was gone. She knew nothing of her dowry. She had no idea what Robert would say when he found out where she'd been for the last few days, prisoner or not.

And then there was Clay.

She took a long breath and dared a glance back in his direction. He was looking away and down at the water, running his fingers lazily up and down Georgene's neck. The angle accentuated the sharp edge of his jaw, brushed with dark stubble. The edges of his loose sandy hair peeked out from under his hat, playing along his ear, and begging her to tuck it into place. She wrapped her fingers in her reins to silence their neediness.

When she thought the silence might destroy her, Clay cleared his throat, a soft but rough sound that perked her up.

"There's something I want you to see," he said as he looked back at her. Crystal blue flecks in his eyes grabbed ahold of her like hooks. "You ever do more than a trot on one of these things?"

It took a moment for her clouded brain to decode what he was saying. "A trot? Well, yes. Some."

A wicked grin met her. "Then let's ride."

His hips and legs moved against Georgene, and she picked up her head, pulling to the left as he coaxed her away from the water. They crunched along the river's edge at a trot. Clover lifted her head with a curious whuffle as the pair moved away.

At first, Sadie just watched them go, stiff hands tugging back on Clover's reins as the mare tried to follow. Then the invitation settled in and registered in her thoughts. He wanted to show her something. Intrigue had her sitting higher in the saddle, coaxing Clover forward. She wasn't sure where they were going, but she was ready to follow him.

As soon as Sadie gave Clover permission to follow, the

horse sprang forward. Sadie clung to her saddle as they broke into a quick trot. Ahead of them, Clay checked over his shoulder, and let Georgene move into a canter. Sand crunched and kicked up beneath her hooves. Then splashing water and crackling rocks as the horses crossed the river at a narrow, shallow section. Both horses hit the far bank and dug their hooves in, climbing the steeper embankment with heaving muscles.

Sadie yelped as she clung tighter to her reins and saddle horn. She'd never ridden so recklessly. Thankfully Clover followed just behind Georgene.

As they crested the top of the embankment, Clay peeked over his shoulder at her with a grin. He was having fun. Seeing his face lit up helped her push aside her nerves and let go. Just because she'd never raced around on horseback didn't mean she couldn't appreciate it.

It was thrilling after all, the mountain of muscle beneath her, cool morning wind in her loose hair. She tightened her knees around the horse's ribs and leaned into their run.

Beyond the edge of the ridge, a wide field opened up, flanked on either side by the surrounding forests. The horses stretched into longer loping gaits. It was much smoother than a trot, and Sadie laughed aloud as she settled into the rhythm, falling in alongside Clay and Georgene. Beyond the thunder of hooves, she thought she heard him laugh as well.

Then he bumped his knee into hers, and she jerked her head to look up at him. An amused grin still laced his face, then he pointed ahead.

A single tall aspen tree stood at the far end of the field, branches of bright yellow leaves swaying in the breeze.

When she looked back at Clay, he bounced his eyebrows tauntingly and leaned over Georgene's shoulders. She sped up, and they pulled away. Sadie opened her mouth in protest, but a smile erupted instead.

If he wanted to race, she'd give him one.

Despite never having the opportunity to run full out on a horse before, she knew how it worked. She loosened her reins and squeezed her knees, asking Clover for more speed. The gray mare's legs churned beneath them, and they closed the gap their competitors had created.

The thrill rushed through Sadie's body like an oncoming train. Wind in her face and loud hoof beats to drown out the blood hammering in her ears. As she and Clover moved ahead, elation surged through her. They were going to win!

Sadie cast a look over her shoulder to see Clay holding back his reins an inch, and she choked out a scowl of a laugh. She hadn't had any delusions she could beat a horseman like him, but she hadn't expected him to let her win either.

She passed the edge of the tree and pulled Clover around in a tight circle to slow her down. Clay did the same, circling Georgene around the tree once before slowing her to a stop nearby and dismounting. Sadie watched him curiously as she caught her breath. On the ground again, Clay strode toward her.

When he reached her side, he offered her a hand. There was a flare in his nose, a rise and fall in the triangle of tanned chest she could see in the open collar of his shirt, that told her the ride had stolen his breath away as well. Something about that sent a flutter through her.

She took his hand and slid out of the saddle. Instead of stepping back and giving her space, he stood still and pulled her body into his on the way down. The shock left her staring up at him with wide eyes.

He moved with a fluid motion that gave her little room for retreat, but she was sure she wouldn't have tried anyway. His fingers squeezed into her waist as he shifted her body, and she found her back pressed into the smooth white bark of the aspen.

His eyes were locked onto hers so strongly she thought she might be lost forever. They pulled at her, demanded her, begged her. When his fingers touched her face, she opened her mouth to speak his name, but her voice was lost when he leaned over her, shrouding her face beneath the dark brim of his hat, and his mouth captured hers.

A shock of electricity hit her instantly. His lips were so smooth and warm, and his oaken smell flooded her. It was nearly too much, but she wanted more. She leaned into him.

What started as a delicate test quickly became a hungry feast. As soon as she reacted in kind, Clay cupped her face to pull her in closer. His head tilted, and his lips explored hers in fervor. With each new movement and caress of his mouth, he pulled new layers of buzzing heat to every inch of her body.

When his lips parted and the tip of his tongue teased her mouth, a gasp shook her. The wet heat was both startling and delicious, awakening more corners of her body. She hesitated only a moment before opening her lips to him. He'd only just slipped his tongue in further when a scream nearby made her jump.

She clung to him in utter shock as she looked around.

At the edge of the forest behind them stood a bull elk, shaking out his thick neck fur and raising his head for another shrill bugle. The high pitched shriek had Sadie shrinking against Clay's chest, and he held her tight there.

"An elk," she whispered. The very beast she and Papa had been searching for in earnest for months.

"Just one," Clay murmured. His breath was short, and she stared up at him again. His mouth was red and moist. She wanted to reach up and plant her lips to it again, but he spoke instead. "But bulls are dangerous during rut. We need to get away from this fellow."

A small part of her thought to beg him not to. To stay and

wrap her in those strong arms again and continue showing her what interesting things he could do with his tongue. The louder part, however, was questioning what the hell she was doing kissing Clay Pearson out in the middle of the forest.

"I've probably kept you away from camp too long anyway," he said. "Soon people will start to wonder where we've gotten off to soon."

For once she wanted to hang her reputation and not worry about what everyone else thought she was up to, but it wasn't a moral society that was judging her purity back at camp. It was her captors, and she was still a prisoner.

Although being a prisoner at the hands of Clay was starting to not seem so bad, and she couldn't help but think so their entire ride back to camp.

CHAPTER 11

Avoiding Clay and those eyes in camp was difficult. She'd spent the rest of the day doing her best not to think of their outing, and threw herself into helping Clara prepare dinner and serve it with a renewed vigor. After dinner, she'd retreated to her tent without a word. Even small talk with Clara was too difficult. She was too good at reading people.

The next afternoon the women busied themselves prepping a hearty lunch for the men that'd gone down to the river to fish that morning. Clay was one of them. Sadie had spent most of the morning both relieved not to be around him and disappointed she couldn't at least catch a glimpse of him across camp.

The afternoon sun peeked in and out of the spotty cloud cover as Sadie cut into a firm tomato. The other women around the fire chatted loudly.

"Don't you worry about hurting his feelings?" Bridget asked as she cut the peel away from a dull red apple.

Ginny plaited her long dark hair over her shoulder. "Of course I do. Jack's my friend. I enjoy seeing him happy."

"You must enjoy it a lot," Clara said.

Sadie sniggered, and Ginny threw her brush at Clara. It bounced off her turned shoulder as the blonde laughed.

"My job is making him happy," Ginny said, turning her nose up into the air.

"But it's not," Bridget protested. "Not anymore."

"Ace doesn't keep prostitutes," Clara directed at Sadie matter-of-factly.

Sadie blinked at Ginny as she tied off her braid. "You're a prostitute?"

Ginny opened her mouth to speak, but Clara interrupted. "She used to be. Now she's one of us."

Ginny smiled sheepishly. "Ol' Joe liked me so much he brought me on home. May he rest in peace."

The three women bowed their heads for an instant before speaking again.

"Then Ace brought you in as part of the family," Clara said. "So Bridget's right. It's no longer your job to make any of these men happy."

"I know," Ginny murmured, "but Jackie's so cute. Even more so when he's happy, if you know I mean."

Sadie lowered her head. She couldn't imagine the life of a prostitute. The very idea of becoming a single man's wife was a big task after living so isolated. Adopting wifely duties seemed paramount enough, but adding on a crew of others? She'd been around Emerald Falls and St. Aspen enough to know men. She'd even stepped foot inside the saloon once or twice. She'd seen the prostitutes and the sea of pigs that fawned over them. She shuddered.

"Sounds like you love him to me," Clara said as she shook a handful of salt into her bowl of tomatoes.

"Making Mason happy makes me happy," Bridget said with a smile, "and I love him."

Ginny shrugged a shoulder and plucked up an apple and

an extra knife. "Maybe I just don't know what love is. You always make it sound so beautiful."

"I think it is beautiful." Bridget gave a dreamy sigh.

"Sure. Mason rescued you. Jack is just...well, you know, Jack. He drinks too much, and he smells a little, but he's a nice guy."

Sadie paused as she cleaned her knife, watching Ginny with a deepening crease in her brow. She'd once thought Robert smelled of cows. She hadn't thought much of it at the time, but things had changed. As soon as her mind flitted to Clay, she was overwhelmed by the memory of his leathery oaken scent. It was enough to carry her off into a memory of the day before.

Clara's voice brought her back. "Just a nice guy isn't going to keep you happy."

Sadie stared at her, recalculating her thoughts. Robert didn't smell bad, and she'd never seen him drink a bit of alcohol. He was a gentleman. He was nice. Wasn't that enough for a good husband?

"A nice man sounds like a good man to me," she ventured. "I can't say I've met many men that glow like a god."

A laugh burst out of Clara, but Bridget sat forward on her barrel with a frown.

"It can be more than that. Some men are special."

Ginny snickered too. "Some have more money."

"No, no. I mean, you can find one that touches your soul in just the right way, you know?"

"Are you sure it was your soul he was touching?" Clara asked with a snort.

Bridget's eyes widened, and she chucked a half-peeled apple at the blonde, who dodged and threw her hands in the air.

"Why's everyone trying to pelt me?"

"Just because you don't believe in love doesn't mean it isn't out there," Bridget said.

Clara's lips pressed into a firm line, and she went back to stirring tomatoes. An awkward silence fell. Sadie's brain whirred. Bridget said she'd found a man that touched her soul in just the right way. The idea both twisted and warmed Sadie's insides.

Lunches with Robert were nice because she got to dress up and go into town. She enjoyed sitting at a table with him, and sometimes his mother or Lilah, and having other ladies look her way, wondering who she was and where she'd come from. Having Robert cut his eyes at her over their meal had made her smile.

But it hadn't made her breath catch or her face flush with a warmth that tickled her skin and her stomach. His eyes didn't snag hers and refuse to let them go like a beautiful blue pair she'd stumbled upon.

Was that what it was like to have your soul touched?

A shiver wiggled up her spine, and Bridget broke the silence.

"I just worry that you might be wasting your time with Jack."

Ginny nodded. "I know, but where am I going to go to find someone else? If I leave this place, I'll have to start working again to feed myself. It'll never work out."

"Something will come about when you least expect it," Sadie said.

Clara caught her eye for the first time that morning and gave her a knowing smile. Sadie cleared her throat, making a big production of wiping her hands on a rag.

"What about you, Sadie?" Ginny asked, smiling a little too brightly as she sat next to her. "Tell us about your fiancé. I bet he's dashing, hmm?"

Sadie pasted on a smile, and her insides rolled over. For

the first time since she found out she'd be marrying Robert, she didn't want to talk about him.

"Of course," she managed. "He's—"

A loud commotion just beyond the edge of the campsite cut off her words and drew their attention.

"I don't think letting her walk out of camp is the smartest idea," Ace stated, his voice lifted high into the air. He stood with his back to them, arms crossed in front of him and shoulders solid and stern.

"She wouldn't be alone," Clay's low voice growled back. Sadie perked up, leaning in the direction of the conversation. "I'd have my eye on her. Besides, she'd be safer with me than leaving her here, and you know it."

The women remained silent, listening with lifted brows and fixed stares.

"You know she's worth a lot of money," Ace said. "We need her back here in the next couple days."

"I'll be sure that she's here. The delivery is the day after tomorrow. Nothing to worry about."

"Don't tell me what to worry about, boy. You just be certain you don't screw this up."

"Have I ever screwed up on you before?"

Ace snorted and rubbed a hand over his face, stepping away for a moment and returning. Sadie could nearly see the tension rising off his shoulders like steam from a hot rock in the morning.

"What's gotten into Clay?" Ginny murmured.

"I don't know," Clara whispered. "I've never seen him buck Ace before. Something's got him all stirred up."

Her eyes met Sadie's for a moment, and Sadie bit into her bottom lip. She busied herself with scooping up peeled apples and dropping them in her bucket.

The men spoke again, this time too low for the women to hear. Sadie stopped moving, straining to catch a word, but before she knew it, heavy footsteps were approaching. She jumped back to the apples, picking up a freshly peeled one and slicing it neatly within her palm, dropping the chunks into a pot of boiling water.

"Miss Tanner," Clay called as he marched up.

She jumped, nearly skewering her skin, and looked up at him.

"Pack whatever you'll need to travel for a few days. We're leaving out in an hour."

Then he was gone, heading off toward his tent and leaving her stunned.

"What was that?" Bridget hissed.

Clara shook her head. "I have no idea."

A tiny thrill wiggled in the pit of her stomach at the idea of traveling with Clay, but he didn't seem too happy about it. Rationality settled over her and tried to smother the tickling feeling inside her.

Where were they going? What was he so mad about? Was she in any danger?

"Do you think I should be worried?" she murmured, looking around at each of the women.

Ginny was the first to purse her lips and shake her head. "About Clay? I wouldn't be."

Sadie looked back down the path where Clay had disappeared into his tent. Logic told her she needed to be careful and make no assumptions, but something in her heart told her there wasn't a thing to fear. Being away from the gang would actually be a relief, and she smiled.

EXCEPT THEY WERE NOT ALONE RIDING AWAY from the gang.

Sadie rode Clover down a beaten path through the woods, behind Clay and in front of Mason. She'd had nothing to pack up as Clay suggested, so she'd had lunch with the girls while she waited for him to return. Ginny had taken a brush to her neglected hair and spun it into a sun-kissed braid down her back. When Clay came back to her, he had horses and Mason in tow.

"I love this time of year," Mason was saying as they plodded along a game trail through the trees. "The air getting cooler, and the leaves turning colors. And all that food? Mmm."

Sadie didn't have to check over her shoulder to hear the grin in his voice.

"My mama used to make up a fancy little feast at the end of harvest, and we'd have pheasant and pies, and my daddy loved those purple eggplants. My mama was the best cook in three counties. I'd eat so much I was afraid I'd pop."

He chuckled and made some more appreciative sounds. The tone of them even pulled Clay around to look. He gave Sadie a sly smile, and she had to cover her mouth to hold in a fit of giggles. Mason didn't seem to notice.

"I'm going to build Bridget a house with a big kitchen one day. She says she likes to cook, but it's not as if we have a proper set up out here in the woods. Maybe I'll find out one day soon that she can cook like Mama."

Sadie looked back in time to see his eyes sparkle. His face was stretched in a wide smile, and his gaze was lost in the trees as they passed. He was in his own world. A warm feeling spread into her chest, watching him think of Bridget.

She'd seen a few girls fawn over boys as she grew up, but she'd never seen the boys do it in return. Not like this. The way Bridget had spoken of love earlier wasn't near as surprising as Mason walking with his head in the clouds.

It was different but alluring.

Where were the men like that in the world?

"Miss Tanner." Clay cleared his throat.

Her breath caught when she realized he'd held his horse back and was riding alongside her.

"Yes?"

"I know Mason likes to talk a lot," he whispered.

"It's fine," she said, a tiny giggle in her breath. "He seems happy."

Clay gave an exaggerated eye roll, but there was still a tilt of a smile on his lips. "He's been acting like that since he came back with Bridget."

"I heard someone say he rescued her. What happened?"

Clay's eyes jumped back to Mason for a moment, and he kept his voice low. "She was being held by another gang. Nasty fellows. She was lucky he came across her."

Even though she didn't know Bridget well, her heart went out to her. Being with the Van den Berg gang had been nerve-racking for the last few days, but her experience had been surprisingly gentle. How bad did a gang have to be for a fellow outlaw to call them nasty? She grimaced into her fingers.

"You think Ace is ever going to leave Ibis Ellard alone?" Mason asked as he sidled up along Sadie's other side. "I mean, I hate him too but it's been nine years. Ace has caused enough havoc to run the guy off."

Clay gave Sadie an exasperated smile. Mason was talking again.

"It has been a lot of chaos, but Ellard hasn't gone anywhere," Clay said.

"Because he's an idiot." Mason shrugged. "I don't mind running the guy into the ground. It just seems like a wasted effort sometimes."

"Except for the money part."

"Except for that."

Clay pulled back on his reins and dropped back along

Sadie's horse's flank. "Take the front up there, Mason. We're almost to the road. Be on the lookout."

Mason slid a rifle out of his saddle and set it on his lap. With his eyes on the move, he fell silent.

"That's better," Clay whispered, leaning forward in his saddle to smile at Sadie.

Her cheeks flushed. The sunlight lit up a handful of shades of blue in his eyes. It wasn't often that he removed his hat, but he'd hung it on the saddle horn in front of him a mile ago, revealing the long sandy strands of hair.

"Where are we going anyway?" she asked.

He sat up in his saddle again, clearing his throat and adjusting his seat. "We've got a job to take care of for Ace. Well, a couple."

The way his eyes moved and didn't come back to hers made her stomach sink. They were up to no good.

"What are they?"

"Our first stop is your cabin."

CHAPTER 12

Sadie frowned, a pulse of shock running through her. "My cabin?"

"Your father's cabin," Clay said. "Ace wants to clean it out. I guess he heard about your engagement and figured you wouldn't need it anymore."

Her eyebrows tightened. "He heard?"

"I didn't say anything. I swear. Not my business to be blabbing."

Her hands tightened on the reins, and she stared at the sway in Mason's shoulders as he plodded along ahead of them on his black Morgan horse.

"What does he want?" she asked after a pause.

Clay shrugged. "Any valuables. That place will be ransacked once you leave. He wants first dibs on the goods."

A sneer curled through her lip. "He could just ask instead of robbing me. In front of my face, besides!"

"Well, you weren't exactly invited along."

Her eyes cut over to Clay. His strong jaw was set, lips slightly pursed, eyes on the road ahead. She hadn't seen him look so lethal before. It was frightening, but thrilling. The intensity in his eyes drew her in, had her leaning a few inches out of her saddle. She started to reach out and place her hand on his arm, but thought better of it.

"What do you mean?"

"Ace didn't want you to go. He wants to keep you close by. You're his piggy bank right now." He rolled his eyes, cutting his gaze over to her. "He was afraid if I took you away that you wouldn't be back in time to make the swap for the money. He set the pickup date in the letter to your aunt. You're supposed to be at the Emerald Falls train station for the swap the day after tomorrow."

She swallowed a knot of nerves. Two days before they realized Aunt Hilda would most certainly not pay a ransom for her. She wiped a moist palm on her trousered knee.

"Is that what the two of you were fighting over?" she asked.

His eyes softened, lips pressed together. "You heard that?"

"Some of it. We all did. The other ladies seemed surprised."

"I'm sure it was alarming. I don't question Ace. He's given me a lot, like all of us, but something came over me. I had this assignment to run for Ace, but I couldn't leave you there. Not alone."

"Clara's there. Bridget and Ginny. They're nice."

"It's not safe. Not with all the others."

His eyes were on the woods again. A wide opening in the trees was approaching ahead of them. They were nearing the road.

Her fingers fidgeted with her reins as she let his words sink in.

Not safe.

The outlaw himself had said it. A small shiver shook her core. Had she been unsafe the entire time?

"Most of the Van den Bergs are good people, don't get me wrong," he continued, "but there are some I don't trust."

Her mind jumped to Tom and his friends torturing the poor fox, and an unpleasant taste spread over her tongue.

"Like Tom?"

He studied her for a moment before answering. "Especially Tom. He takes without asking. He's not equipped to be around civilized people."

An image flashed in her mind of the first time she'd seen Tom's cold dark eyes, peering out above the black bandana covering his face. The blood in her veins ran cold.

"So I'm here then?" Her voice barely topped a whisper.

The muscle in Clay's jaw flexed. He ran a hand through his bronze locks. She clenched her reins tighter, wishing she could do the same.

"It took some convincing," he said, "but Ace relented and said you could come with me. I guess I had a better ultimatum."

He'd argued with Ace on her behalf? Something fluttered in her chest, and she pressed her palm against it. Her pulse pattered against her fingertips. No one had ever been so concerned about her well-being. Her father had been a good, hard-working man, but he'd had no qualms about hiding her out in the woods with him after her mother passed away. It'd been a lonely and laborious childhood. The abandoned ache in her chest confirmed what she'd always known. It hadn't been the right choice for her. It'd been cruel, and she'd always resented him a little for it.

Clay, on the other hand, hardly even knew her and was fighting for her against an outlaw gang leader.

Her neck and cheeks flushed at the thought.

He wasn't like any outlaw she'd ever heard stories about.

She waited for a beat in hope he'd elaborate on his ultimatum, but he rode on in silence.

"What about the assignment he sent you on?" she asked, adjusting her focus. "What is it?"

"An interception. We're going to reroute Ellard's mail."

"What do you mean reroute?"

"Ellard is a sheep farmer. He ships sheep as far as Texas. He has a big establishment—"

"I've heard of Ibis Ellard," Sadie said. She was proud to know anyone in town, even if he wasn't a particularly decent man.

She'd studied the families in Emerald Falls from afar as a child, learning their names and stories. The information she didn't know, she made up, developing elaborate stories of their pasts and turning each into a fully-fleshed person in her own mind. Even if she knew little of the truth. She drew in a lot of hearsay from customers at the general store or Papa's vendor site. Once a week they'd spend an afternoon selling their tanned hides and apricots, and then she'd visit the store for their weekly wares. Unfortunately, she didn't see the townspeople much more than that.

"Then you know he's a wealthy man," Clay said.

She nodded.

"Unfortunately for him, he's also not very smart. He ships all those sheep third party and doesn't trust his delivery team. So the pay for the sheep comes by mail."

"You're going to steal his money?"

Clay paused, rolling his tongue against his teeth. "We're going to relieve him of the extra funds he obviously does not need, yes."

She scoffed. "That's just plain stealing."

"Maybe, but he owes Ace a little money too, and he refuses to pay."

His eyes didn't falter. There was no twitch or tell in his muscles to make her believe he was lying.

"Why does he owe him money?"

Clay rubbed at the back of his neck with a half shrug. "Ace and Jeremiah used to work on Ellard's ranch. Years and years ago. Ellard didn't take care of his boys. Didn't pay them right. They worked like dogs and didn't get taken care of proper. Things really came to a head one night and half of Ellard's hands split. A fence got broken. A lot of sheep got loose. Ellard paid some of his loyal boys to track down the offenders and get rid of them."

Her voice trembled as she spoke. "Get rid of them?"

Clay nodded, jaw tight. "Yep. Two of the hands got shot, killed. Ace cut one off before he got to Jeremiah. Didn't end well for that fella. But then Ellard got the law involved. Thankfully Ace outsmarted them. It was a big mess though."

A mix of emotions yanked their way through her chest. Destroying Ellard's inventory and livelihood was wrong. Stealing his cash money was wrong, but ordering death on people, especially ones you treated like slaves, was inexcusable. If he was as wealthy as Clay implied, and as she'd heard around town, then he had more than enough money to employ healthy and satisfied ranch hands.

"I can see why Ace is so angry," she said.

Ahead of them, the trees tapered off into an open stretch of fields and a red dirt road running north and south.

Mason drew his horse up and pulled his hat down to shade his eyes. "Which way, boss?"

Sadie stopped her mare behind Mason and lifted in her saddle to look past him, trying to gain her bearings. Then Clay's fingers were on her elbow. They were rough but gentle and ignited a spread of warm goosebumps across her skin. She looked at him, memories of the last time he'd touched her flooding back. His eyes were deep, dark, and hazy, and something told her he was thinking of that moment too.

Then he nodded his chin down the path to the right.

"Emerald Falls is that way. Which way to your cabin?"'

With an uneven breath, Sadie looked around Mason to the path again. She recognized a group of trees and the last three posts of an old dilapidated fence. She pointed to the north.

"It's a few miles back that way. Not far."

Mason continued onto the road. In the back, Clay let his fingers slip away from her arm. Her skin felt empty without him.

The horses shuffled forward as a group, their hooves dragging onto the red dirt road.

"You live a fair way out," Clay ventured. "Was your daddy a rancher?"

She scoffed under her breath. "That would be a better reason, wouldn't it? He had some sort of self-inflicted isolation he stood by. We don't own much land. Just a small cabin."

"It's not so bad being away from town."

Clay's face was relaxed as he stared down the path ahead, a content tilt to his eyes and lips. As if he truly believed the sentiment. The very idea hurt her chest.

"Sure, if you had anyone else your age to talk to. Or anyone besides your own father even." Guilt immediately twisted her gut, and she bit her lip. "I mean, he was a good man, my papa. He took care of me. He bought me things when he had a spare nickel, but for the most part, it was more important to him to live out here than to let me be close to people."

"Was he hiding from someone?"

She shook her head. "No. People in Emerald Falls seemed to like him just fine. What little we saw of them anyway."

"So he had some other secret."

Her back straightened like a feather-ruffled turkey. "He had no such things. He was a simple hard-working man.

We worked together. There was nothing to have secrets about."

Clay lifted one shoulder in a lazy shrug. "Sounds like a man with a secret to me."

"Maybe he just likes the peace and quiet out here," Mason offered.

Sadie wanted to thank him for his interruption on Papa's behalf, but Clay cut in first.

"Raising a bored child? That doesn't sound like peace and quiet."

Her mouth set in a firm line. "I didn't complain." At least not too much.

"It's okay, Miss Tanner. Children need interaction. A parent is not enough. Sometimes even a sibling isn't enough."

"What about your mama?" Mason asked. "Did she like living out here?"

Sadie shook her head. "Mama never lived out here. We only moved from town after she died."

Mason hid his grimace under a hand, rubbing fingertips over the dark stubble on his chin.

"It takes a strong woman to survive without her mother, I imagine," Clay said.

"I was eight. Just a child. I remember her, of course, but it didn't affect me as much as when I was older. I missed her a lot more. It is hard with only a father around," she agreed.

"Good on him for raising you so well."

Her nose wrinkled. "You don't even know me. I could be a mess."

"Maybe not," Clay said, "but you're no mess. You've been through a lot in the last few days. Kidnapped. Lost your father. Had to bed down in a campsite with a bunch of lowlifes." Her head snapped around, shocked he would put such words in her mouth, but he was grinning. It eased the frustration from her bones, and she smiled back.

"It hasn't been all bad," she ventured.

A familiar darkness fell over his eyes, and his voice dropped to a lower tone. "I'd hope not." The fire in his eyes had her taking a ragged breath, wishing she had a paper fan to cool her neck with. She must have amused him, because he countered with a hearty chuckle. "I mean, we've got some scruffy fellows back there. But—"

"But I wouldn't shy away from all of them." The words just fell out, and Sadie's tongue ran over her dry lips.

One of his eyebrows twitched, and his grin grew. "That right?"

"Well, I mean, I agree. The lot of you are a bit scary. I didn't know what to expect." She cleared away a sudden nervous grating in her voice. "But you're not scary. I was a bit shocked to find that out, actually. Who knew that there were outlaws that weren't exactly undesirable?"

His eyes sparkled. "You think I'm desirable?"

The heat that rushed into her face nearly took her breath away. She turned her burning cheeks back toward Mason and the road ahead of them. The veer off to her cabin was nearly upon them.

Thank goodness.

She cleared her throat and urged her horse to pick up the pace. "We're almost there."

Clay and Georgene hurried to ride along at their side.

"That's refreshing to know," he continued. "That I'm not the scary outlaw you thought I was. You know, I thought you were a prissy city girl."

She glowered. "Really?"

"Sure. Pretty dress. Traveling on the train from the city. Your hair was done up nice. Throwing a fit over sleeping on the ground. You looked like any other city girl I've met."

Frustration steamed out of the collar of her simple cotton shirt. She wasn't sure what was worse, the way Clay made "city girls" sound so bad or the fact that she'd always dreamed of living in a big community. That she aspired to be the dreaded city girls he spoke of.

"Well, I'm not," she spat.

"I know. You shoot guns and you're wearing pants." He laughed aloud. "Ain't no city girls doing that."

She glanced down at the clothes she'd borrowed from Clara. It wasn't what proper ladies wore, she knew, but she was so used to them that she hardly noticed.

"I see it," Mason said. The horses perked up, jumbling together as they funneled down the narrow path to the cabin in the woods.

"This is it," Sadie said, glancing once more at Clay as they neared.

His good humor had faded into a concentrated face as they approached. He was back to working at what he did best, she assumed. Scoping things out and thieving.

The horses nickered as they grouped up next to the hitching post in the center of the lawn. Clay gave Georgene a pat on the neck as he took a look around the clearing and the late afternoon sun filtering through the trees.

"The evening's coming. Let's see what we can get finished before nightfall. Mason, you want to check that the coach is still running on schedule for tomorrow?"

The other man frowned beneath the low rim of his white hat. "Back in Emerald Falls?"

"Yes, sir."

Mason looked between his companions and cleared his throat with a firm nod. "I'm on it."

The big black Morgan horse tossed his head with a snort as Mason heeled him back out onto the road. The two disappeared in a cloud of red dirt and hoof beats.

Once he was gone, Sadie peered at Clay silently.

They were alone. For the first time since their morning out by the river.

Nerves buzzed through to her fingertips, and she turned her body to throw her leg over Clover's back and dismount. Clay was still watching the opening in the tree line where Mason had departed. Beneath him Georgene stomped a hoof impatiently, blowing wide nostrils.

Then Clay's eyes were on Sadie, piercing right through her body and into her soul. He dismounted in one smooth motion and rested his hands on his hips.

"Guess we can get to packing things up while he's gone."

She looked back to the cabin with a new flutter of nerves. "There's really not much here. Just some hides and a few rations for the winter."

"That's just fine, Miss Tanner. We'll let Ace know we got what we could."

Clay pulled an oatcake from his saddle bag. As he let Georgene nibble the treat from his hand, Sadie walked along the front side of the cabin to the door. It didn't look any different than it had when she'd left it days ago, but it was strange being back without Papa. It would seem so large and hollow without him there.

She pressed her palm against the thick wood of the front door and pushed it open. As it cracked open from the frame, a musky stench hit her. She grimaced, peering inside. Across the large open room, sunlight fell inside through the frame where the back door had once stood. It hung in cracked pieces by one remaining hinge.

Sadie gasped, eyes darting around as she stepped inside.

The room was a long rectangle, a doorway on one end leading to her bedroom. What was usually a tidy living space was in shambles. The wood table in the middle of the room was turned on its side, one leg broken off, and the former contents scattered across the floor. Papa's bed tucked into the corner was nearly broken in two. On the far wall, the crates that used to hold their winter stores were destroyed. Ravaged vegetables and rations were tossed in all directions.

The air reeked. An animal had gotten to their supplies. Sadie felt deflated as she turned to call out to Clay.

Something shifted in the dark corner opposite the open door. Her breath caught in her throat as a giant grizzly bear turned its massive form around to growl at her.

CHAPTER 13

Sadie shrieked and stumbled back across the room. She fell over a broken chair with a gasp. Furniture scraped and moved as the bear wheeled around and charged.

She pulled herself back over the debris. There was no way she could outrun a bear. Papa's rifles were propped next to his bed, too far for her to reach. She was going to be crushed, eaten alive in the house she grew up in.

Her shoulder hit the overturned table. It was heavy and blocked her path. She cowered against it with a scream, throwing her arms up to shield her face as the grizzly rolled its giant body off the floor onto its hind legs and roared.

"Sadie!"

Clay's boots came thundering inside. Gunshots went off above her head, and the bear bellowed. She clutched at her ears, another scream scraping up her throat as she ducked away from the chaos.

Another pop of a gun. Sadie looked up just in time to see one of the bear's massive paws rip into Clay's jacket. The force nearly dropped him to the ground, but he managed to swing his revolver around again for another shot.

The bear snarled, turned on its tail, and ran. It pushed its way out of the broken back door and was gone nearly as fast as it'd appeared. Sadie fell back against the table with a gasping shudder.

"Sadie." Clay's voice was strained. His hands were on her arms, pulling her to her feet to face him. The sharp crease in his brow and the hollow void of concern in his eyes made her heart quake. "Are you okay?"

"I think I'm alright. It just—I didn't see it. I—"

She felt outside of her body, still watching and running from the bear. It was difficult to slow down. The nightmare was over, but her drumming heart and shallow breaths still ran like a train.

Clay's hands slid up her arms and shoulders to press into the back of her neck, holding her closer, and she found solace in his warm, firm touch. It pulled her back from the edge of panic and wrapped her in a blanket of hope.

Her eyes darted over his face, desperate to see him. To know that both of them were still alive. In whole pieces. Escaped the wrath of an angry grizzly bear.

The very idea of being trapped in the same room with a grizzly sent a fresh shudder down her spine.

But she was alive.

Clay had saved her.

She pressed her palm to his cheek, searching his eyes as she fought to control her breathing.

His chest rose and fell in a deep rhythm that betrayed how frightened he'd been as well. She traced her fingers along the exposed edge of his collarbone through the opening of his shirt, skin she'd wanted to touch for days. As her fingertips grazed his flesh, his eyes clouded, and his hand slid into her hair.

"I thought that bear had you." The husky breath in his voice tickled the nerves throughout her body.

"I'm still here," she breathed.

Something primal flashed in his eyes. "Thank God. Here you are."

His fingers tightened in her hair, and she gazed at his soft lips, skewed in concern. She'd dreamed of touching them again since their kiss near the river. It was as if they were beckoning her, and she was in no state of mind to deny her desire.

She pressed a kiss to the firm line of his lips. They molded to hers instantly. She fell into his arms, overcome with relief and fueled by a fire ignited deep within her.

His arms crushed her against his body with an urgency she returned, sliding her fingers into the soft hair she'd been dying to feel and pressing herself into him. Needing more of him. Wanting every inch of her body to be covered with his warmth. Craving the firm muscles that melded into her.

Clay's mouth was hot on hers, falling into a rhythm that melted her insides. She'd never felt so vulnerable and safe at the same time. He'd moved far into territories she was unfamiliar with, but she couldn't stand the thought of him being anywhere else.

He teased her lips apart, and she opened up to him with a passionate sigh. The shock of his warm tongue on hers sent her pulse fluttering. For a moment her breath was gone, and she leaned back an inch to look at him.

She expected to find his normal flirty smile, but what she found drew her up tighter than a bowstring. There was no smile on Clay Pearson's face. Only a strong jaw, soft lips, and intense eyes. The look melted her against him, and he claimed her mouth once more.

The rumble in his body was deep, growling and possessive. The feel of it against her chest and mouth strummed a string deep down in her body she'd never reached before. A wet heat that surged through her and met between her legs.

The exchange between them was curious and tantalizing. She could make a big, strong man like Clay growl with need, and he could take over her body and make it do things she could not.

It was strange, and she liked it.

Testing her own power, she moved her tongue against his, flicking and dancing. He tasted of a savory sweetness she'd never found in any food she'd eaten. It was more delicious and satisfied her in a way no meal ever would again.

He groaned. The throbbing in her core intensified.

His hands were possessive in her hair, cupping the back of her head and drawing her in. She welcomed it, leaning into him, and lifting off the ground to hook a knee around his leg.

It was all the encouragement he needed. He dipped and hoisted her up into his arms. She gasped against his lips as he tucked her in close and moved further into the dim light of the cabin. It was as if she floated weightlessly across the room until her back came in contact with the wall. He pressed her into the wooden panels with the weight of his body. Her legs spread to wrap around his waist, lodging him in tightly against her core, and it jolted a live wire within her.

When his lips left hers, she opened her mouth to protest, but all she could manage was a hollow gasp as his kiss trailed down the tender skin of her throat. Hot mouth and teeth on her neck and the edge of her shoulder sent her pulse tripping. Her fingers slid up the back of his head into his hair, running through the long strands, just as soft as she'd imagined them.

One of his hands moved up her body to tug at the neckline of her shirt, exposing her collarbone. Muscle memory insisted she cover it immediately, but his mouth moving over the tender skin demanded she let it be.

When his fingers popped a button on her shirt free,

however, the voice in her head screamed a warning. No one had ever undressed her, much less a man in the heat of passion. Her nerves fired, begging her to stop him. This was a dangerous act. She was being much too risky. Especially with the company at hand. And yet, it was the company that swept the thoughts away. She felt safer than she ever had. Clay Pearson would not hurt her.

She closed her eyes as he trailed a set of kisses over her collarbone. Then he inched out a second button.

His fingers against her skin were soft, and his mouth on her sternum was like a prick of fire. When he breathed soft words against her, her mind went blank, and she wrapped tighter around him.

"You smell divine, Miss Tanner."

A sudden itch coursed through her fingers. She wanted to see those eyes again. To see him staring back at her.

Her fingers tightened in his hair, and she pulled back.

He froze, fingers slipping free of the buttons on her blouse and nothing but his breath left upon her chest. When his eyes met hers there was a concern there that tugged at her, and she pressed her free palm against his cheek, letting it contour to the evening stubble that had sprouted along his jaw.

"It's Sadie," she said.

Then she smiled, and all the tension in his face disappeared. The depths of his eyes grabbed her, just as she'd hoped. The lopsided grin on his face was brilliant and fueled the fire within her before his mouth was on hers again. Hungrier, intense in a way that nearly shocked her, but she met him with a growing appetite.

His hands moved into her blouse, popping threads and shucking the garment down her shoulders. He trailed kisses down her chest and onto the top swells of her breasts. Her breath caught, tantalized by the tingling through her body.

He lifted her back off the wall and moved through the single doorway into a small bedroom. Her room. She clung to him, but she needn't worry. His strong hands were around her bottom and holding her like he might lose her at any second. She tightened her legs around him, her thrill heightened in knowing that would not be the case, and he groaned against her lips.

The primal sound he emitted awoke even more corners of her body, and she squirmed against him. His fingers flexed deep into the muscles of her behind, and she gasped.

The bedroom was much darker, but she knew what was in there. A simple end table and a bed. Before she had a moment to register being in the dark with him, Clay had lowered her shoulders down onto the bed. His lips trailed down her sternum as he let her go, inch by inch. The heat from his mouth on her chest clouded her mind.

With her legs still wrapped around him, he leaned over her lowered body and moved his hands to her camisole. As her eyes adjusted to the dark, she could just make out his fingers moving, and buttons popped free in rapid succession.

His moist breath was on her chest again, trailing to one of her breasts. Goosebumps broke out over her skin.

Then his lips closed over the taut peak of her breast, and the nerves in her belly leapt. Fire spread through her chest and down into the junction between her legs, pressed in tight against Clay's body. She writhed against his mouth, and his tongue teased her sensitive skin.

He moved to the other breast, sucking and teasing until she pulled in a ragged breath. Then he lifted away. His strong hands kneaded into the skin at her waist as she slid the rest of the way down onto the bed. When his fingers met the hem of her pants, he slid them a few inches down her hips.

Her fingers dug into his back, a small flicker of panic darting through her.

Clay's hands stopped. He rested her fully onto the bed and knelt over her. Then his hands were gone. Fabric rustled, and a whoosh of air moved over her half uncovered body, drawing the damp tips of her breasts up even tighter.

In the fading light, she could see the hard lines of Clay's bare chest and arms. She reached hands out to touch the firm stomach over her, hard and soft at the same time, with a patch of coarse hair beneath his belly button. She hadn't expected that and ran curious fingers through it, tickling at his skin. The hum in Clay's throat was deep and wicked. His hands rested on hers, guiding them to the brass belt buckle at the front of his pants. Her breath caught as her fingers passed over the cool metal and the straining seams beneath.

A knot of nerves gathered in her throat, but the soft caress of Clay's fingers on hers kept her grounded.

"I've got you, Sadie," he whispered.

The sound of her name on his breath stirred a renewed desire within her, and she took hold of his fingers. He moved his hands over hers as he unfastened the buckle. It snapped in the darkness as it fell away. She slid her fingers along his sinewy forearms as he worked, admiring the way the muscles moved, before his hands were on hers again. His palms covered hers entirely as he pressed her fingertips into the loosened hem of his pants just behind his hips.

There wasn't much holding his pants on any longer. One of her fingertips edged beneath the hem, pushing her boundaries and smiling at the thought of it. Then more fingers, and she slid the pants down his body. Her hands pressed into the tight muscles of his bottom. She never knew touching another's body could feel so good. And exciting.

Clay's pants fell away, and he reached for her. His hand slid up her shoulder, her throat, into the hair at the back of her head. Then his hungry mouth was on hers, tasting and teasing. Her lips burned as he crushed into them, but she welcomed it. When he lowered his body over hers, pressing against her along the way, her hips lifted from the bed to meet him. She couldn't get enough. She needed him closer. She wanted to pull him deep into her core.

This time when he rested a hand on her hip, she pushed it down to the edge of her pants, begging for more.

His whisper was deep and rumbling against her lips, just her name, but it was enough to drive her wild.

She lifted her hips higher as he pulled her pants down her legs. In a flurry, he sat up to yank her boots free and rid her of all extra garments. She lay still beneath him, waiting for him to cover her once more with his warm body.

His hands traveled up her thighs, over her hips, and caressed her breasts as he knelt over her again. His kiss pressed her deep into the bed mat as a hand slid down her torso to the apex of her body. His fingers were cool against her burning core, and a delicious shiver coursed through her.

When he edged her thighs apart, she spread before him, searching to quench the urges within her. He fit himself against her and took her mouth harder. She could hardly breathe when he sunk in deep, and a cry of surprised ecstasy escaped her lips.

All the years of searching to belong, to feel right in the world, vanished in an instant. Nothing had ever felt as right as Clay.

She moved her hips up to press into his, greedy for more. A groan rolled in his throat. The sound made her even hungrier, stretching and reaching, needing more of him.

His lips crushed into hers as he moved within her. The bruising pinch against her mouth was sharp but perfect. Her hands were lost in his hair, twisting and pulling as he turned her body into a liquid fire that burned through her center and out her limbs.

She tasted him with her tongue and lifted to meet his

movements, falling into his rhythm until he growled. When one of his hands snaked around her hip to cup her bottom, pressing her ever tighter into his body, she thought she might explode. A waterfall of heat coursed through her, and she cried out, clinging to Clay's slick body. Muscles clenched and tightened in a euphoric frenzy that left her faint. He moaned against her lips as his body did the same, and she clung to him in surprise. When his body relaxed, he slid down to the bed next to her.

They lay for a silent moment before his arm went around her and drew her in close.

Sadie's muscles trembled, and her mouth was sore, but the small prickles of pain felt too glorious to worry over. She rested her head against his chest and closed her eyes. She hadn't known such a level of contentment existed, lying there in Clay's arms with her body aglow. She felt as if she could close her eyes and sleep for days.

CHAPTER 14

Lying with her cheek pressed against Clay's hard bicep gave Sadie a drowsy smile. Her fingertips slid up his forearm to his wrist and back to the elbow, gently exploring his skin. Not ready to break the warm connection between them.

Except the bothersome cool air was tickling her thighs and her belly. All the spots that had felt as if they were on fire just moments ago were quickly feeling the chill. Reality ebbed its way into her brain once again, and the thought of lying there with no clothes on made her throat contract.

She was naked, tucked in close to a naked man.

Nerves bounced about within her. She needed to find her clothes. She couldn't be lying around the cabin without them. What if Mason were to return?

Her throat squeezed tighter.

Mason could return at any moment. He'd catch her in the nude. Even worse, in bed with Clay. She pressed her lips together until they ached.

Clay's stomach growled.

She popped up as if it'd bitten her.

"I'll see what's left of the food," she said as she slid to the edge of the bed.

His fingers trailed down her spine as she moved away, eliciting a delighted shiver. She turned back to look down at him. Just the edges of his long hard body were lit by the last of the evening sun through the window. Even the edge of him was beautiful.

She gave him a lazy but happy smile before getting up.

"I hope there's a bison out there," he murmured, sounding nearly asleep. "I'm starving."

She chuckled. "If there is, the bear brought it."

He grunted a drowsy laugh as she slipped across the room. She squinted in the darkness as she crept. The sun had disappeared in a rush. How long had they been in there? Little to no light filtered through the window.

She felt around the floor with her barefoot until it touched the small chest near her bed. She opened it and pulled out some clean clothes. Anything would do. She dressed in a better fitting blouse and a similar pair of brown woven pants. The clothes didn't sit quite right at first. Her body felt moist and worked in a brand new way. It was odd, but she loved it.

Once she was covered again, she moved about the cabin with a calmer energy. Out in the main room, she went to the nearest shelf and pulled down a candle and matches. The sharp smoky smell of the lit match covered some of the rotten bear stink, and she set the small flaming candle on what was left of the kitchen counter.

The bear had destroyed the hutch full of rations in the corner. Broken cabinet doors lay on the floor with cans and what was left of the fresh vegetables scattered about. All the jerky and dried fruits were gone.

Sadie tiptoed through the remains of half-eaten carrots and around a large glass shard from a broken jar of preserves. Among the pile of tin cans, she pulled out some beans and an intact loaf of bread. She touched the tip of her nose to the crust and drew in a breath. It was hard, but it still smelled fresh.

It would do.

She stepped wide and crossed over to the kitchen counter, swiping some wood splinters and food debris onto the floor with her sleeve. A small box on the counter looked untouched, and she smiled. With a flick of her finger, she popped the wooden lid and lifted out a roll of hard cheese.

She was just opening one of the cans of beans when a boot crunched behind her. Before she could turn her head, long warm arms encircled her. She grinned as Clay's chin rested on her shoulder and his nose rubbed at the tender skin below her ear.

His bare chest pressed into her back, his warmth enveloping her. She leaned into him as she worked, letting the newly familiar scent of him surround her. His body on hers was like pieces of a puzzle. It fit just right and made everything all the more clear.

"Looks like you found something," he growled into her ear.

Her knees wobbled, and she clutched to one of his arms. Even just the sound of his voice could disarm her, and she loved it. His hot breath caressed her ear lobe just before the edge of his teeth nibbled. She folded around him with a giggle, and he rewarded her with a deep, dark chuckle.

The butterflies in her stomach at the smallest touch made her feel like an excited young girl, but the rugged and raw energy Clay put off made her feel like something else entirely. Like a desirable woman. Not one that had been left to grow up alone in the forest with little interaction or feeling of belonging.

She no longer felt lost wrapped up in Clay's arms.

His lips had just dipped below her ear to smooth down her neck when the sound of hooves approached outside. The ragged breath that blew across her collarbone was laced with both agitation and amusement.

"He has the worst timing," Clay grunted.

His arms slipped down her body and fell away as he walked back to the bedroom. His dark pants rode low on his hips, but he was still shirtless. Sadie eyed the tawny back muscles and the smooth slope of his waist as it disappeared beneath the hem of his pants. Her tongue ran along the inside of her lips as she recalled the feel of her hands on that skin. Caressing, molding to him, pulling him closer.

Clay Pearson was a delicious man.

Just as he was disappearing into the bedroom, there was a knock at the doorway. The door was missing, so there was no mistaking Mason standing just outside. Sadie leaned over the food with a smile tugging at her lips, hiding her blushing cheeks as she called out.

"Come in."

Mason's boots crunched through the mess, and he let out a low whistle.

"What happened in here?"

Sadie found a knife on the kitchen counter and sliced into the bread. "Bear ransacked the place."

"He sure did, and left his mighty stank behind for us. Whew."

"Not to mention he ate half the food and ruined the other half. Thankfully I did find some things for us to eat."

"Excellent. I prefer not to eat the jerky rations unless I have to. Where's Clay?"

"Here."

Clay emerged from the bedroom, shirt in place and belt buckled. He looked just as he did every other day, except for the extra twinkle in his eye. The crease at the edge of his mouth when he smiled. The strong arms and rough but gentle hands. Those lips that could ignite fire.

Sadie's body twitched, and she snatched her eyes away, focusing on cutting the bread and cheese. It was impossible to look at him and not leer. She cut her eyes over one more time before forcing herself back to work, scooping out some beans and creating a few sandwiches.

"Find any information?" Clay asked.

"A ledger confirming the money delivery tomorrow. It seems everything is on schedule."

"How did you get a peek at the post office's ledger?" Sadie asked.

Clay stepped up to the counter where she worked on the food, and his hand brushed hers as he gathered the empty cans. Her eyes popped up to his, gazing at him beneath her lashes. The edge of his eyebrow perked as he smiled at her, and it took all her willpower not to throw down the sandwiches and kiss him again.

She nearly forgot Mason was in the room, his voice sounded so far away.

"Ladies like my smile."

She frowned a little, looking back at him over her shoulder. He grinned—it certainly was dazzling—and popped the edge of his hat in the air.

"Evening, ma'am," he drawled with enough charm to smother a horse. "Might you be willing to give me directions to St. Aspen?"

Sadie's face broke into a grin at the reenactment. He was good. His green eyes and bright smile were enough to make any woman stop and look.

She propped a hand on a hip. "It worked just like that, did it?"

"Oh, sure." Mason straightened the collar on his shirt. "A little smile, a little lean over the counter with a pouty lip. Drives 'em wild. She fetched me a map, and I took a peek at her book there. Easy as pie."

"Mmhmm," Sadie murmured, crossing her arms over her chest delicately. "Does Bridget know that's how you get stuff done?"

Clay's chuckle next to her was low, meant only for her.

Mason's grin didn't falter as he took a seat on the only chair still standing.

"Sure, she does. We all have our talents. But she ain't worried about me."

"Why not?"

A light twinkled in his eye as he shook his head. "No offense, Miss Tanner, but Bridget Steele is the best lady I've ever met. She hung the moon in my sky, and she won't let me forget it." The tips of his ears flushed, and Sadie pressed a couple fingers to her lips to hold back her giggle.

"Doesn't sound like she has too much to worry about after all."

"No, ma'am."

Clay cleared his throat as he stepped up behind Sadie. Quite close. She could feel one of his legs on the back of her thigh and his fingers sliding against the small of her back. She glanced up at him, suddenly so close she had to crane her head. His eyes were heavy-lidded, sultry.

"I don't know about you, but I'm starving," he rumbled.

Her body slackened, leaning back against his chest. He moved an arm around her, strong fingers closing on her arm. When a wicked grin curved his lips, she snapped back to the present.

"Oh, right. Food," she said as she slipped out of his grasp and opened a low cabinet near the kitchen sink.

"Whatever you've got smells good," Mason said.

What they had was cold food, but she supposed he'd eat anything that wasn't the dried rations in his saddle bag. She pulled out a stack of plates and served up the sandwiches. When she held one out for Clay, she found him wrapped in the wool blanket from her bed.

"Thank you," he said as he took the plate, then swung his blanketed arm toward the door. "Mind if I sit out on your front porch?"

"Of course. It's not any warmer in here anymore."

"If you want warm, you should feel this blanket I found back there on the bed. It's like a furnace under this thing." He gave her a small wink as he turned, and her insides melted.

She had her own furnace burning already, but she couldn't deny the urge to hop under the blanket with Clay. To feel his body against hers again.

She gave a quick glance to Mason as she handed him a plate, and he averted his eyes.

"Starving," he murmured under his breath as he took a bite.

Her back straightened, and suddenly she didn't care about Mason's opinion any more than he wanted to give it. She marched for the door and stepped out into the darkness.

Clay sat on the thick wooden chair where she'd seen her father sit on many occasions, whittling wood or telling stories about Mama. The memories of being a young girl, sitting on the edge of the step and listening to Papa's words, were drowned by the image of Clay. He leaned back in the chair, draped in the blanket like a royal chieftain. His large form filled the chair like Papa's never did, and she stared at him in silence.

When she didn't move, the corner of his mouth crooked up, and he tilted his chin up an inch to beckon her over.

Her legs moved of their own accord, and she was at his side in a few steps. They slid together as if they'd done it every day of their lives. She sat astride his knee, leaning back against his chest, and he wrapped her in the red and black wool.

They were silent a moment as they ate. She hadn't realized how hungry she was until she took her first bite. It took only moments for them both to devour the sandwiches.

"Thanks for the food," he said, setting their plates aside. "My brother used to make bean sandwiches for me."

Sadie's nose twitched. "You mean Tom? I can't imagine him doing anything nice for anyone."

Clay's chest shook her as he chuckled. "I know. He's pretty rough on the outside, but he was a damn good older brother."

"Really?"

"Sure. He took care of us after our mother left. I doubt I'd have survived without him."

"By himself? How old were you?"

"Five I think. Tom was seven. Technically my mother's Aunt Mae was caring for us, but things were rough there. Her husband was an evil man."

Her fingers tensed against his arm. She forced them to move again, drawing long lazy circles against his arm.

"Evil?"

He grunted a low reply. "Cut from Satan's belt itself. The man loved whiskey. Couldn't function without it. Unfortunately, we were often in his way."

She stared off into the trees behind the grazing horses, spines lit by the soft blue glow of the moon. Living with a drinking guardian sounded horrific.

She wanted to give her deepest sympathies, but she was

sure nothing she said would ease his past pains. Instead, she twisted to look up at him, rubbing her nose up under his chin as one of her hands found its way into his hair. She trailed her fingernails delicately along his scalp, and a shiver moved through his body.

"I'm sorry you had to go through that," she whispered.

The blanket shifted, and his fingers eased along her jaw, caressing her cheek and teasing her lips.

"You grew up without a mother too."

"I did, but I had a father that cared for me."

"Enough to hide you away from the world."

Emotion knotted in her throat. "He changed after Mama died. I'm not sure what drove him to the woods. She loved it out here, but she was also well-known in town. I doubt she would have moved while she was alive." She shrugged. "It was unfortunate, but I never doubted that he cared for me."

Clay's lips turned up, and he pressed a soft kiss to her mouth. "I'm glad you never felt unloved."

She smiled against his lips, and he pressed his forehead to hers.

"What happened to her, your mother?"

"She got sick. Pneumonia. Papa never really talked about it much. She just got sick and was gone so fast."

He nodded gently, head still resting on hers. "I'm sorry."

"I would ask him. I wanted to know more about her, but he got really sad when he spoke of her. One day he caught me trying on one of her dresses. I don't know why we still had them. Something in him changed after that. He treated me more like an adult. I think that's when he started trying to figure out how to get me back to Emerald Falls."

She hadn't considered how he would go about making that happen until he brought home the news.

The very thought of Robert and Papa's arrangement made her insides squirm. Ice filled her chest, and she snuggled deeper into the blanket. Clay didn't speak another word, only pulled her closer into his chest, and they watched the wide expanse of starry sky through the trees.

She'd been so excited by the marriage proposition in the beginning. It was her ticket back to town. Sure, Robert was dull, but he was a gentleman. He lacked a few notches in bravery, but he was respected in the community. His father was definitely someone everyone wanted to know.

It had been the perfect opportunity to integrate herself back into the lifestyle she missed so much.

Until the afternoon on the train.

In just a few days, her world had been turned upside down. She'd gone from wanting to run back to her life to being swept off her feet by the very man who'd stolen her away.

The longer she was away from her old life, the more she'd doubted Robert would take her back. And the more time she spent with Clay, the more she was sure she didn't want him to.

As if she'd spoken the words aloud, Clay came to life beneath her, and his breath touched her ear.

"You can do better than Emerald Falls, Sadie Tanner."

She turned to look up into his deep blue eyes. Barely a glimmer in the darkness, but they still reached for her.

No matter what else was to happen in her future, she felt quite content in her little cabin in the woods. Normal for the first time in her life. Desirable. Come what may with Aunt Hilda's money and Robert's judgment, she would lose herself in Clay for as long as she could.

His hands slid beneath the edge of her shirt, rubbing into the soft skin of her waist. Any confusing thoughts that had been clouding her mind grew fuzzy and disappeared. Then his mouth found hers, and it was doubly difficult to hold any rational thoughts in her head.

He kissed her with a strength that took her breath away. Then he twisted her beneath the wool blanket to slip an arm beneath her knees and hoisted her up against his chest as he stood. He cradled her in his arms and strode across the porch. Nothing else existed in her world as he stepped back inside and carried her to her bedroom.

CHAPTER 15

Sadie tied a second bundle of pelts onto Clover's back. Her saddlebags were already stuffed full of the last of her clothes and some of the surviving cans of food. Georgene and Mason's gelding were loaded down with animal pelts as well.

The morning sun streamed through the tree limbs, leaving a patchwork of light over the horses' coats. Sadie looked up into the clear sky, the steam from her breath puffing lightly into the cool air, and smiled. Most of her worries from the night before had been put to rest when Clay had scooped her up in the blanket and taken her back to her bedroom. He'd worshipped her body again, and she, his. The dance hadn't been as foreign as before, but it was no less enjoyable. She'd slept like a rock in his arms afterward.

"That's the last of them," Mason said from the porch.

She gave him a wave of acknowledgment as she checked the rope on her hides.

Mason had slept on Papa's bed in the main room. The three of them had spent breakfast nibbling on some canned peaches and not meeting one another's gaze.

"I think that's it then," she said.

She'd collected her belongings and everything they could, knowing she might not return to the cabin again. It would be abandoned. For now. The land did technically belong to Papa. She could get in contact with someone in town about selling the place. After disclosing that he'd passed on. She didn't want to face that part.

"Good. Grab Clay. We need to head out."

Sadie climbed the step to the porch and stuck her head inside the cabin door. Clay stood near Papa's bed, a stack of papers in hand. He shifted one back, reading intently. When she stepped inside, he looked up.

He ruffled the papers. "Have you seen these?"

She lifted a shoulder as she approached. "What are they?"

"Letters. Your pop kept letters from everyone."

A melancholy smile twitched in the corner of her mouth. "I didn't know that. Where were they?"

"Stashed in the corner under his bed. You should probably read them."

The tone in his voice perked her eyebrow. "Why?"

He paused, and his eyes searched her face.

"Just interesting exchanges between your parents is all. I'm sure you'll enjoy it."

A more genuine smile came over her, and she nodded. "Thank you. I'll bring them along. Mason's ready to go."

Clay wrapped the papers up in twine and stuck them back into an old paper sleeve.

Sadie took one last look around, said her silent goodbyes with a glimmer of moisture in her eye, and followed Clay outside into the sun.

Mason was mounted up and waiting near the edge of the clearing. Clay walked with Sadie to her mare and tucked the stack of letters into the recesses of her nearest saddle bag.

Then he offered her a hand and helped her up onto the horse.

"Beautiful morning," he said, rubbing his thumb over her knuckles before dropping her hand. "Nice day for a little financial reassignment."

Despite the morbid implications, she laughed aloud. His grin grew.

"Busy day ahead of us," he said, voice lifted so Mason could hear him as well. He grabbed his hat from Georgene's saddle horn and climbed up. He settled the black hat on his head, low over his eyes, and nodded. "Let's get a move on."

Mason heeled his horse out onto the road.

The three of them left the cabin and the clearing behind, turning out onto the main path. The road split the forest for half a mile before it spread out into wide expanses of green prairies and long straight roads. Mason took the lead while Clay trotted at Sadie's side.

She loosened the thick jacket collar at her neck as the sun crested the mountains in the distance and warmed the air. Soft white clouds stretched across a robin egg blue sky. A gentle breeze touched Sadie's cheeks and stirred her hair.

It was a perfect morning.

The horses had settled into a peaceful gait, and she stole a glance over at Clay just in time to catch his eye. And a dark smile.

Georgene moved close enough to bump Sadie's leg, and Clay's hand moved over to take hers, resting against her thigh. Despite the warming air, his hand felt hot. She squeezed it lightly.

Ahead of them, Mason glanced back at them. When his eyes fell on their hands, Sadie's first instinct was to let go, but Clay's fingers wove into hers with a finality that sung in her heart. Rather than hide, she sat a little taller in her saddle.

Mason's brow knit slightly as he turned back to the front. He spoke without turning again.

"Let's keep our head in the game today. There's a lot at stake."

Clay grunted a halfhearted chuckle, then set Sadie's hand aside. At first, she was disappointed at his reaction, but the firm set in his jaw and brow said he wasn't casting her off. He had other matters to tend to.

He nudged Georgene forward and flanked Mason, giving him a solid chin-nod.

"What's the problem, Kent?"

"Nothing. We just need to be sharp. You know that."

"I'm fine. I'm here. Let's do this."

Mason cast a short peek over his shoulder at Sadie and spoke in a hushed tone. "You're not fine. You've got your head in the clouds back there."

Clay's head lowered an inch, the rim of his hat casting a shadow over his sharp eyes. "You think because I fancy a lady I can't stick to a plan?"

Butterflies set off in Sadie's stomach. As if the previous evening with him hadn't been any indication, the words on his lips sent a thrill rushing through her. Even if he was using it in his defense.

"I just wanted to be sure, is all. You're like my brother, Clay. I ain't going to let some woman endanger you."

Clay turned toward the road ahead of them without a word, and Sadie shrunk inside herself.

She didn't want to cloud his judgment either if their plan involved something so dangerous. She considered asking to stay back at the cabin, out of his way and where she would provide no distraction, but a fear tickled at the back of her neck. That bear could come back, and she'd be all alone.

She grimaced and rolled a shoulder up to rub at the shiver in her bones.

Ahead of her Clay glanced at Mason and reached over to shove him in the arm. Mason rocked in his saddle but remained upright.

"I appreciate the sentiment," Clay rumbled, "but just because you're the fastest gun in Wyoming, don't mean the rest of us can't take care of ourselves."

Mason drew back and punched Clay in the shoulder. Sadie jumped, hands flying to her mouth in surprise.

Clay rolled his arm with a grunt and a grin.

"You're lucky I'm in a good mood, or I'd have to shootcha."

Mason grinned back.

Sadie stared in confusion. The men looked suddenly lighter, less rigid. Mason turned back to her with a smile on his face.

"We'll have just enough time to sell skins before we kick off the plan. Do you have a regular customer?"

Her brow creased, trying to keep up with the conversation's directional change. "The general store picks up a stack or two sometimes, but usually we sell to individuals. Hank Lawson will buy up a big lot of elk at the end of the season, but we don't have elk this year."

Mason exchanged a glance with Clay.

"We will try the general store," Clay said. "No harm in trying there first. We just want to move them." He eased up on his reins and let Georgene drift back in Sadie's direction. "We can take less than you usually sell them for. Just get rid of them."

Sadie frowned. "Papa and I worked hard for all these skins. Why would you just dump them?"

The edge in Clay's eyes eased. "It's not to devalue your efforts. Ace sounds like he's going to be on the move soon. We can't be hauling a pile of furs around with us. We just need the money."

Sadie's breath slipped out of her lips with a ragged sigh. The logic was sound, but it didn't make the idea hurt less. The last harvest of skins she'd made with Papa would just be gone, like they didn't matter at all.

Clay's knee brushed hers as he fell back in beside her.

"After that, we'll be off to our target spot. We'll find a place to hide near the road. It's wooded on that side, plenty of brush and trees to hide behind. Once the coach comes by, Mason and I will get to work. You can lie low until I get back."

Sadie's fingers fidgeted on her reins. "Is it dangerous?"

"There's always a chance for danger, but as long as you lay low, you'll have nothing to worry about."

"It's not me I'm worried about."

His eyes fixed on hers as he drew in a breath deep enough to move his chest. He reached over and trailed the back of his finger down her temple and jaw.

"I'll be just fine. We're not going in guns blazing or anything."

She leaned into his hand before he let it fall. "No one will get hurt?"

"That's the plan. I'll provide the distraction. Mason will pick up the delivery. We'll all walk away unscathed, and Ace will have his money back."

Sadie wasn't sure she entirely understood the morality in the money exchange, but the most important aspect was the three of them remaining safe. She couldn't stomach the idea of Clay walking into a gun fight.

"Hopefully everything will go off without a hitch," Mason said. "I'll drop these furs off with you, then I'll run by the post office. We can meet up here on the edge of town."

He nodded toward the first wooden posts of an outlying corral. Noisy sheep and pigs rooted in the muddy pens that lined the east side of town. A couple of livestock handlers stood next to the fence with papers in hand, pointing at the animals and counting aloud, preparing them for the next train ride out.

Beyond the livestock yard stood the first buildings on the main road. A doctor's office and a bank. Across the street stood a tavern and the general store. Further down beyond view would be more shops and businesses.

People moved up and down the dusty road, on foot and on horseback. Sadie recognized many faces, but none looked her way. Even though she'd seen most of the residents of Emerald Falls throughout her life, she'd spoken to few since she was a child. She didn't even know if they knew who she was.

When a woman glanced up at Clay and Mason as they passed, Sadie's palms began to sweat. Of all the gang-related occurrences happening over the last few weeks, she had no idea which one of them had been the Van den Bergs. Robberies on the roads going in and out of town, horse theft, pickpocketing passengers on a stagecoach.

Not to mention the train robbery she'd witnessed firsthand.

Had those incidents been these men? Had it been Clay Pearson?

The addicting eyes and strong jaw of the man at her side drew her gaze, and her stomach rolled. If he'd done any of those things, would people of the town recognize him?

The woman didn't say anything as they passed, and Sadie's lungs ached as she let out a breath. She averted her eyes as they continued to the main path through town.

Brown's General Store was the second shop on the north side of the strip. Mason turned onto the main road, but Sadie cleared her throat.

"They take deliveries in the back," she said, a slight waver in her voice. "We should go to the rear entrance."

Mason nodded and pulled his horse around, skirting the saloon at the front of the shop line, and leading the way to the backside of the buildings.

She bit into the edge of her lip, keeping on the lookout for anyone that paid them too much attention. Thankfully there weren't many pedestrians out that early in the morning.

The backside of the store strip was empty, and they hitched the horses outside the general store's back door.

"You think he'll take it all?" Clay asked as he dropped to the ground and pulled down a stack of skins.

"He's never bought a quarter of this many," Sadie said.

Clay stopped next to her to offer a hand. She glanced around, finding a sudden blush itching up her neck, and accepted his fingers in hers as she slid off her horse.

"Thank you."

"Don't worry. We won't be here long."

His fingers slid up the outside of her arm as she unloaded a bundle, and she conjured a smile through the ill feeling in her stomach.

Something about being back in Emerald Falls had made her insides feeling heavy and sick. After so many years of being excited to go into town, she was completely thrown off. She'd put so much energy into making sure she clawed her way back in, only to have it shattered upon the floor like crystal.

Being there that morning, sneaking around in the shadows with the Van den Bergs, turned everything upside down.

Mason set a stack of furs in the dirt next to the door and went back for more. Clay hovered at her elbow with his load.

"Just give him a price," he said as she approached the door. "As low as you want. We'll work through it."

She nodded. Her throat was parched. She rubbed a hand

over her itchy neck as she knocked on the door. She waited a breath, then opened it.

"Mr. Brown?" she called, swallowing the dry crack in her voice.

Something shuffled near the front of the store. She stood just inside the door, the bundle of furs cradled against her, and hoped Mr. Brown wouldn't recognize her. As if she'd look as different as she felt.

When Mr. Brown came around the corner, his eyebrows went up.

"Miss Sadie Tanner? What on earth are you doing back here?"

Mr. Brown's eyes darted back behind her, and Sadie froze. Boots hit the wood floors behind her, and she could feel Clay come to a stop near her. Her muscles clenched, breath caught in vice-like lungs.

The store owner would recognize him. How could he not? Clay looked nothing like the people of Emerald Falls. Strong and handsome, a hard stare that could rip you apart or bring you to your knees. The very thought of it made her insides quake, but it couldn't touch the pain in her stomach. The fear that Mr. Brown would know Clay.

Yet, she wasn't sure which would be a harder reality for her to face. Being caught with a known outlaw, or Clay being recognized for the unlawful things he'd done.

Mr. Brown's gaze jumped back to her, and she swallowed.

"I have furs," she stammered. "A good lot of them."

Mr. Brown frowned and looked down at the stack of pelts in her arms. "Miss Tanner. You know I only take a half dozen of these small ones a week. You have an awful lot there, and there."

He narrowed his eyes as he looked to Clay again. Her heart hammered in her ears.

"I heard you've been missing a few days," he said.

Her pulse tripped. People had realized she was gone? She adjusted the furs in her slick palms.

"Robert Murphy was in here just yesterday telling me that you'd disappeared." Mr. Brown's eyes twitched, narrowing a fraction further as he regarded Clay.

Her heart slammed against her ribs. She wanted to wheel around, push Clay out the door, and run, but her body was frozen. She couldn't even see Clay's face, but the scrutinizing one on the shop owner was enough.

"Was he?" she croaked.

The sharp eyes popped back to her, and she jolted.

"He sure was. Poor lad's worried sick. Glad to see you back in town. I hope you've gone to speak to him."

Was that empty feeling in her gut guilt or dread? She tried to force it away.

"But I see you've been taken care of," Mr. Brown continued. "This fellow a friend of yours?"

She didn't think. She didn't consider any alternative but to escape.

"Of course not. I pulled him off the street to help me unload."

Even an entire step ahead of him, she could feel Clay flinch.

CHAPTER 16

"That's right," Clay grumbled. "A mere acquaintance she just met. Ain't no need to worry about this pretty lady tangling up with a roughneck like me." Clay stepped alongside her to hold out the stack of skins.

Sadie felt so small as she looked up at him, folding in on herself as she searched his face. It was rigid around his smile. A fake pleasantry as he tried to coax the shop owner into taking the goods. She wanted to apologize with her eyes. To stare into him and tell him she hadn't meant it. He was so much more than an acquaintance. Hell, he was so much more than any other person in her life.

But he wouldn't look at her. He left her gazing at him in near-teary frustration.

Mr. Brown had moved on after her comment. He waved at the bundle Clay held out.

"I don't need all that. I'll take my usual. Maybe a few pieces more. That's it."

Clay cleared his throat. "I believe she mentioned these are deeply discounted. Far below fair price."

His elbow nudged her shoulder. Despite the sting in her

cheeks, she stepped forward with a nod. "That's right. Half price. I'm selling out of my stock, Mr. Brown. This is all of it."

The shop owner pursed his lips as he stared at her. "How much do you have?"

Clay set his bundle on an empty counter and disappeared.

"Quite a bit. Mostly small game. A few cougars. I need to get rid of it today."

"Why such a push? Your pa ain't sick is he?"

For an instant, she considered telling the truth, but Papa's death was far too mixed up with Clay. It was risky. Instead, a quick lie fell out of her mouth instead.

"No. He's leaving town. He doesn't want to work in pelts anymore."

"Going back home to St. Aspen, eh? I can't believe it took this long."

She pasted on a smile, though behind it her heart broke a little. She missed Papa, but the idea of him leaving town was nearly as painful. Had he wanted to go back to St. Aspen all along? Where he'd grown up and the last of his family resided?

She swallowed the lump of emotion in her throat. "Yes, and we don't need to take these with us. A quarter of the price, Mr. Brown. I need them gone."

As he looked the skins over, rubbing thick fingers along his pale beard, Clay returned carrying two more bundles. Mr. Brown's eyes widened a fraction, but he didn't speak. A strained silence followed. Then he dropped his hand with a sigh, reaching for the pelts in Sadie's hands.

"Are they all the same good quality? I must admit I get compliments on them, even if they don't move quickly."

A weight lifted from Sadie, and she smiled weakly. "They are. The same as ever."

Mr. Brown opened the bundle and flipped through a few

of the furs before setting the stack on the counter. "Fine. I can take them at a quarter price."

She hadn't believed they would sell. Not so much at once. It was hard to contain the relief that shot through her from her head to her toes. She wanted to jump into Clay's arms and hug his neck, but she couldn't do that in the store. Mr. Brown was already much too suspicious of her. Instead, she helped stack the skins and took the offered dollar bills with trembling fingers.

"Thanks, Mr. Brown," she said. "Have a blessed day."

"Tell your pa it was good doing business with him all these years, and I wish him the best."

She gave him a tight-lipped nod on the way out the door.

Outside she let out a long breath, glad that part of the morning was over. Then her eyes jumped to Clay. There were so many things she wanted to say to him, but he was already at Georgene's side, pulling the reins up over her head.

"Hey," Sadie called gently, hurrying to catch him. "I'm sorry about—"

"Don't be silly," he said as he swung into the saddle. "You did what you had to do."

"No, really. He cornered me. I just didn't—"

He turned, nearly bumping her, and put his hand on her arm. For a moment, she was relieved to feel the warmth of his skin, the familiar calluses on his palm, but the depth of his eyes didn't swell when he looked at her. They were beautiful but disheartened.

Something inside her broke.

"Don't worry about it," he was saying. "We need to find Mason over at the post office. It's time to ride out."

He unhitched her horse and settled the reins behind the saddle horn, dusting off the seat for her. Then he helped her mount up.

"The coach will come through in about an hour. We need to be in position before that."

With a quick hop, he pulled himself into Georgene's saddle and urged her forward. Sadie followed. The buckskin mare tossed her mane with a nicker, picking up to a trot as they came around the corner of the shops.

Sadie's stomach churned as she watched Clay's broad shoulders ahead of her. She hadn't meant to hurt him, but Mr. Brown's stare had tied her up in knots. What would he do if he thought she was running around with an outlaw? Would he send for Robert? Or call the sheriff? She broke out into a sweat just recalling his sharp eyes.

Worse yet, what would he do to Clay?

They passed by the saloon in uncomfortable silence. It was quiet at that time of the morning. An older woman stood on the wrap-around porch, sweeping with a short straw broom. She glanced up as they rode alongside the building and made their way across the main road to the outlying post office at the head of town.

Mason's horse was hitched out front next to a fancy white stagecoach. Rust-colored train tracks ran parallel to town on the opposite side of the building. A few birds sat on the railway signs lining the tracks, and a pair of older gentleman leaned over a game of cards near the front door. One had just slapped down his cards with a devious grin when Mason strode out the door with a small stack of paper in his hands. His face lit up when he saw them.

"I don't see any furs. I hope that means you have money." He grinned at Clay.

Clay shifted in his saddle without a word, then edged his eyes over to Sadie. The tips of her ears burned as she reached into her pocket. She'd been so preoccupied with chasing Clay down to apologize that she'd forgotten all about the money.

She slipped the stack of bills from her pocket and held them out to Clay.

"We sure do," he said, voice low and gruff as he took the money and held it up.

Mason looked between them with a small twitch of his brow. "That's good. Ace will be happy to see that. Now." He checked the dial on an old brass watch in his pocket. "It's about 8:15. We best scoot if we want to intercept these guys before the nine o'clock drop off."

They turned the horses toward the west, riding out the opposite end of town from which they'd arrived. The long red-dirt road stretched through massive plantations and miles of wood fences.

"You won't have to associate with such lowlifes much longer, Miss Tanner," Clay said, his eyes fixed on the road ahead. "After we finish up here, we'll take the money back to Ace. Then he wants us to ride on out to your aunt's house."

Sadie frowned, her heart dropping into her stomach. "What?"

He remained still in the saddle. "We didn't hear back from her by his final date. Guess he thinks she's holding out. So I'm taking you down to St. Aspen and, I don't know, standing outside her windows with you to collect the money. Guess I forgot to mention that before."

Her heart sank even lower.

"You're going to parade me around like a prize pony and demand money from her?"

He lifted a shoulder, finally looking over at her. The beautiful spark in his eyes was gone, and her chest tightened. A wash of hurt enveloped her, but anger burned at the edges.

"Fine. You get your money. Do whatever Big Ace tells you to do."

The muscle in his jaw tensed.

"Ace does what's best for all of us. If he thinks taking you down to St. Aspen is the right choice, then that's what we'll do."

She rolled her eyes and focused a hot gaze on the back of Mason's jacket. She didn't want to see those empty blue eyes. How could they go from so alluring to infuriating in a morning's time?

They rode in silence, only passing one other rider on the road. Past the farms, the only place the road led was St. Aspen. It was likely they wouldn't see many more people before the coach arrived.

"This looks like a good spot," Mason said, slowing his horse in the road and circling around.

A small clump of trees sprouted near the path. Huckleberry bushes grew around the trunks, providing enough cover to hide the horses. And Sadie.

"Duck down in there next to the horses," Clay instructed. "We'll move farther up the road to meet them. You should be safe back here."

She grit her teeth. "Wouldn't want your piggy bank injured."

His lip curled in a half-snarl as he pulled Georgene up next to her and reached a hand out to touch her face. She flinched, but his palm cupped her, a thumb sliding over her cheek as the tips of his fingers edged into her hair.

She cursed the oaky scent that enveloped her, the urge she had to press a kiss into his palm. The way her head swam at his touch, and how she nearly forgot her anger.

"Don't sell yourself short, sweetheart," he murmured. "You're still worth money injured."

Some of the blood drained from her face, but a bigger fire burned in her chest. She swatted his hand away.

They dismounted and hid the horses in the brush, giving them each a carrot to munch on, and Sadie settled herself in the shield of the berry bushes.

"Just keep quiet," Clay whispered as he peered through the brambles at her. "No matter what you hear up here, don't come out."

Nerves flickered throughout her chest, but she nodded.

When he'd gone, she set her jaw and grumbled.

Still worth money injured.

Sadie hugged her knees to her chest and blew out a long breath. Maybe it would be a safer bet to go along to Aunt Hilda's, no matter how awkward and unwelcome the encounter would be.

At least she wouldn't be at the mercy of Ace Van den Berg's greed. Or Clay Pearson pulling at her heartstrings.

She huffed out a sigh and crossed her arms over her chest. As much as she wanted the anger in her to burn through the rest of her emotions, pain grabbed at her. Her heart ached. She'd been so happy that morning. A woman on top of the world.

It'd been smashed with a look and words so indifferent that they took her breath away.

Where had her Clay gone?

She closed her eyes and took a long breath. She wished Papa was still there. He was such a smart man. He'd be able to work out all of her problems.

Except he'd be horribly disappointed in her. Her stomach rolled at the thought. He'd worked out a nice arrangement for her, and she'd spoiled it.

Above her Georgene and Mason's horse shifted and bumped about, looking for more carrots. The buckskin mare poked her nose into Sadie's hair and blew out a warm breath. Sadie rubbed her fingers along the horse's nose. As the beasts bumped and leaned apart from one another, Mason's saddlebag shook and dropped some papers.

Sadie pulled them out of stomping hoof range. One was

addressed to Jeremiah back at camp. The other to Ace himself.

In Aunt Hilda's handwriting.

Sadie gasped, her fingers tightening on the letter so quickly she nearly crumbled the thing into a ball. She jerked her head around for check for spectators. Mason and Clay were a quarter mile down the road already.

Her fingers trembled as she turned the letter over. There was Aunt Hilda's address on the back of the smooth white paper.

Sadie's tongue felt much too dry and her eyes wide as she slipped a finger beneath the blue seal and snapped it loose.

Georgene blew out a whuffle of breath when Sadie popped her head up for another quick peek. The men were gone, but not far from where she'd seen them last, a coach was rolling down the nearest hill toward them.

She squatted low again as she opened the letter.

There were very few words on the page. A formal address and a signature enclosing just two lines. Even the long and elegant pen strokes weren't enough to ease her nerves on what the sentences would contain.

Dear Mr. Van den Berg,

I appreciate your gentlemanly nature as to inform me of Sadie Tanner's whereabouts, in case others may be in search of her. I regret to inform you, however, that no one in this household claims a Sadie Tanner, and I will not be sending my own family's money in order to fetch her.

Do have a good day,

Hilda Tanner

The letter lowered in Sadie's slack hands as the words pierced her like knives.

She knew the woman wouldn't send help, but she hadn't expected the cruel, indifferent words Aunt Hilda had written.

No one in the household claimed her.

It didn't matter that it was only Hilda and her spindly butler that lived in the big house in St. Aspen. It still hurt to hear.

Someone shouted down the road, and she popped her head up. The coach had stopped, and the driver was on the ground, fretting over someone in the road. Her heart stopped.

Clay lay in the red dirt, and her chest clenched.

"Sir, are you okay?" The driver's voice was frantic even over the distance.

Georgene blew a hard breath into Sadie's hair.

"There's a snake in there. It bit me!" Clay shouted, writhing on the ground.

Sadie's mind snapped back to the plan he'd discussed with Mason. It was a show. A distraction.

She ducked back down into the brush and stuffed the letter into her pocket.

It was no matter that Aunt Hilda didn't want her. Or that Clay would rather sell her off for money than keep her around. She didn't need any of them. She just needed to vanish before they realized their ransom scheme was botched and they no longer had use for her.

She stood and snatched Clover's reins from the cluster of trees and pushed her out of the brush. The gray mare tossed her head in surprise but backed away as Sadie instructed.

A nagging feeling pulled at the edge of her consciousness, but she pushed it away. Clay and Mason were bringing back their intercepted mail money. Ace wouldn't need her anymore. It wasn't as if they were going to get any more money for her anyway.

Sadie pulled herself into the saddle and yanked her reins around, spinning Clover in a tight circle. They sprang from the brush.

Someone shouted down the road. Then a gunshot.

Sadie gasped, wheeling around in a panic. Clay stood firm in the road, pointing and yelling words she couldn't make out. Mason was ducked behind the corner of the wagon as a second coachman shot into the air. The scene was chaotic, and fear for their safety made her nerves falter. She wanted to run to their aid, but she had no weapon. No way to offer any assistance.

Besides, it was her one window to get away before everyone knew Aunt Hilda had refused to pay for her. There wasn't time to hesitate.

She heeled the mare into a gallop, ducking through stray limbs until she was on the open road again. There was no way the group behind her didn't see her, but she didn't look back. Just forward down the long road back to Emerald Falls.

Back to the only person left in her life that made any logical sense.

Robert Murphy.

CHAPTER 17

"Why Miss Sadie Tanner, I've been looking everywhere for you." Robert gaped at her. "What on earth are you wearing?"

Sadie grimaced and looked down at her dusty pants and damp, wrinkled shirt. It was a stark difference from the cleanly pressed checkered shirt and dark trousers he wore, standing in the open doorway of the Murphy ranch house and staring at her as if she'd just been dragged in by the cattle.

"I had a little mishap back there," she said, jerking a thumb over her shoulder. "I lost my dress, and I—"

Robert waved a hand. "It's quite alright. Let's get you some new clothes. Leeann."

A sharply dressed woman with white gloves and a cleaning rag appeared in the archway across the room behind him.

"That's not necessary," Sadie said. "I have some—"

"Leeann, get Miss Tanner into the guest room and draw her a bath. She's going to need some extra clothes."

"Oh, Robert. Really. I don't need all that."

"Nonsense. You'll feel much more up for talking once you're clean and comfortable" His smile took up his whole face, one she'd always found quite charming. This time it twinged one of her nerves.

"Don't you even want to know where I've been?"

"Of course. I'll be waiting for you in the sunroom."

Leeann reached for her elbow and tugged her from the foyer. Sadie jerked away, slapping a hand against the closing front door.

"My horse," she gasped.

Clover, loaded down with the last items she had in the world, stood hitched just outside. The animal's ears swiveled as she peered back at Sadie.

"I'll take care of it," Robert said, snapping his fingers and waving a ranch hand toward the mare.

A young boy, about twelve by the look of him, scurried out from around the side of the house and went after the horse.

"All is well." Robert flashed another grin at Sadie, and Leeann put coaxing fingers on her again.

Sadie wanted to yank free of her, but a bath also sounded amazing after days of sitting around a campfire. With a defeated sag in her limbs, she let Leeann lead her away.

AFTER A SOOTHING WARM BATH, Sadie dressed in a soft blue dress adorned with lace and wavy ruffles along the hem. It was beautiful, but she couldn't help but feel out of place. Nothing she owned was as nice as the dress he'd given her. Nor as starched and hot.

Even with the gentle breeze tickling her ankles as she walked, the dress didn't breathe any better than a cat in water. She took up the blue lace fan that had been sitting out with the dress, the one she'd laughed at just moments earlier, and began to fan herself in earnest.

"You gave us quite a fright, Miss Tanner. Just disappearing like that." Robert handed her a cup of tea, and she paused, reluctantly setting her fan aside to take the saucer.

"The circumstances weren't exactly intentional."

"Yes, I heard about the train robbery." He sat in the wooden scroll chair across from her. "That was devastating news. Especially after no one aboard knew what had happened to you."

She paused with the teacup touching her lip. His eyes were soft and sincere-looking, locked on hers.

Devastating.

He'd said the news was devastating.

Because of how awful it'd been for the townspeople of Emerald Falls? Or because she'd gone missing?

Mr. Brown did say Robert had been looking for her.

She took a small sip of her tea. It was bitter, and she fought back a grimace as she set the cup in its saucer.

"It was certainly frightening at the time," she said.

"What happened? Two hooligans held up an entire train?"

Her back teeth clenched together as she gingerly slid the teacup onto the low table in front of her.

"Something like that. They lifted some valuables. I don't think they got away with much."

Except for her.

Robert shook his head. "No matter what they took, they shot a man. They disrupted the peace of train passengers. Those men should be hanged."

She adjusted her skirts, fanning some air underneath to cool her legs, as she dug for something else she could say. Something that wouldn't paint a big red X on Clay's back.

"You're right. They're scoundrels, those Croakers."

"Croakers did this?"

Her brow creased, and she lifted a shoulder casually. "Who else would do such a thing?"

"I've heard word of other gangs nearby. They could be getting bigger and bolder. Some of them could be worse than the Croakers."

She tucked her fingers into her lap, pressing the toe of her dress shoe into the floor to keep her knee from bouncing.

"That could be, but I know I heard some mention of Croakers when we were getting off the train."

Robert tilted his head with an alarmed perk of his eyebrow. "Why did you get off the train?"

"We, er, well, Papa and I were taken. By the men. They forced us off the train."

Robert stood and crossed over to the settee in one long stride. Her insides clenched as he slid in next to her, much too close. His hand hovered near hers but didn't touch.

"You were kidnapped?"

Her voice came out in a breathy squeak at first. She cleared her throat, dropping a shoulder to lean away from him. "Yes. They took us off the train, but we—we got away."

"How?"

Her breath caught in her throat. How? She lowered her face into a hand, pressing her fingers around her eyes. It had been a traumatizing experience at the time. Terrifying, being ripped from a train. But it seemed so far away. The Clay she knew was not the same man that had demanded she jump from a moving car.

Although the Clay she thought she knew was also not the one who would sell her off to a woman who cared for her as much as she cared for a wad of horse manure on the bottom of her shoe.

Robert's hand rested on her shoulder, and she suppressed a shudder.

"There was some shooting going on," she managed to

whisper. "Maybe the sheriff, I'm not sure. Shooting at those men. It was chaos. Papa and I got away, but we got separated." She coughed, dragging her hand over her face. "I don't know where he ended up. I searched for a few days. Hopefully, he'll just come back here."

She saw Robert nod out of the corner of her eye. "Maybe he will. I'll be sure the sheriffs get back out to comb around for those degenerates. Stealing young, lovely ladies around here. Who do they think they are?"

Sadie bit the inside of her lip. She knew she should be just as horrified it had happened, but she couldn't conjure up quite as much disdain.

She shifted closer to the edge of the couch, collecting her words to ask to be excused, when a commotion came through the front door. Sadie leaned to the side just enough to peer into the foyer.

A short round woman with a brown lace dress and a bob of dark hair rushed in.

"Lands sake, it's true," Mrs. Murphy coughed, staring at Sadie with wide eyes as she strode into the sitting room. "Someone in town told me they'd seen you. I thought they'd done lost their minds. Where on earth have you been?"

Sadie's frame hardened, but her insides turned to mush. The woman's scolding tone was not quite the welcome she hoped for.

"Kidnapped," Robert said simply.

Mrs. Murphy's eyes did not relax. "Kidnapped? Good heavens, by who?"

"Croakers."

The woman shifted forward to position herself more in front of Sadie, pinning her with hard eyes. "Is that true?"

An uncomfortable heat rose up inside Sadie's dress, and she glanced at the blue lace fan on the table next to her. It was too far to grab nonchalantly. She'd have to suffer Mrs.

Murphy's gaze without it. She swallowed a knot of nerves and clenched her hands in her lap.

"Yes, I was kidnapped."

"By Croakers? I've heard such awful stories, especially with young ladies. Did any of them force themselves on you?"

Sadie recoiled, horrified by the suggestion.

"Mother," Robert chided.

"What?" the woman spat, blinking innocent eyelashes. "You know it happens."

Sadie knew it did. It wasn't as if she hadn't been terrified of the possibility upon arriving at the Van den Berg camp. She had been. But Clay had been there to protect her.

The way Mrs. Murphy blurted the words out with a furrow in her brow, however, made Sadie squirm.

"No one forced themselves upon me," she said, doing her best to relax her jaw.

Mrs. Murphy stared at her for a full two breaths before nodding. "It's good to see you back in one piece, dear. I'm sorry you had to go through that."

The flat voice offered no sympathy, but Robert smiled just the same.

"I've had Leeann prepare a room for her so she can rest," he said.

Mrs. Murphy lifted her chin, staring down at them with a haughty expression. "That's a fair idea. I'm sure she'll need to recover after her incident."

The sticky heat of Robert's hand and hip against her vanished as he stood. She felt cooler, less rigid without him next to her. Sitting with him on the settee didn't use to be so uncomfortable.

Mrs. Murphy's eyes on her didn't falter, however. Sadie wanted to raise a hand to her face to block them out, but she kept her fingers clenched at her sides as she stood and followed Robert past the short woman and out of the room.

He led her down the hallway to an open door. Inside was a single bed, dressed in soft blankets and extra pillows and flanked by two wooden dressers. A beautiful porcelain bowl and pitcher sat atop one chest of drawers, and her dirty clothes sat folded on a short wooden stool in the corner.

"We've got new satin sheets on that bed. Take all the time you need for a rest," he said. "I'll have them hold a plate of food for you from dinner if you sleep through."

Despite the awkward tension that thrummed through her, she was thankful for Robert's hospitality. He'd always been a gentleman.

"Thank you. I appreciate you letting me stay."

He snorted a laugh. "You expect I'd turn my fiancée into the street?"

The word sent a jolt up her spine.

"Well, no. But—"

"Where else would you go? Your papa isn't at home. You have no other family. Thank goodness you have a betrothed to go to."

Her muscles tightened, and she put a hand on the edge of the open door to steady herself. Her teeth set, and it took all her remaining energy to force down the anger erupting inside her.

"I can survive well enough in my home by myself," she said, despite wanting to yell it.

He stared for a silent moment, reading the energy leaching out of her eyes. Then he smiled, that darn honeyed smile that swept some of her tension away.

"I'm sure you could. You're a strong woman."

Her fingers twitched on the door.

"A lady must be if she wishes to survive this world. Now, if you'll excuse me."

He bowed his head as she eased the door shut. Once he was gone, she hovered next to the crack in the door and listened as he rejoined his mother down the hall. Mrs. Murphy spoke in harsh whispers, mentioning something of the "truth" and a "dowry." Then the voices moved off too far to hear.

Sadie pushed the door closed until it latched, then pressed her back to it and drew in a long breath.

She didn't know all the details of her dowry, an outdated tradition Papa's wealthy family still practiced, but it apparently had been generous enough to keep the Murphys interested in her even after her disappearance.

Thank goodness, because it was saving her in her time of need.

Of course, she could survive alone. If she had to. Even if it would be lonely and dangerous.

Although the thought of living in the cabin she'd shared with Papa without him broke her heart. Not to mention the bed she'd shared with Clay. Pain pricked the corner of her eyes. She brushed it away with an angry hand.

Living alone at all would break her Papa's heart.

He'd tried so hard to get her this deal so she'd never be on her own. Or stuck in a wooden cabin in the forest for the rest of her life. He wanted her in town. Where she'd always wanted to be.

It wasn't as if she could count on Clay staying safe and surviving long enough to protect her. Papa had been her rock for over a decade, and he was gone. Unlike her father, Clay put himself in dangerous situations daily. Who knew how long that would last?

She stared up at the ceiling.

With a ragged breath that almost hurt to draw, she moved over to the bed and climbed under the blankets. She cuddled down deep and closed her eyes.

No matter what had happened over the last few days, she knew her place. No matter how much she was missing Clay already and wished she could find him again, she knew she certainly would not be welcomed into Emerald Falls with him.

She needed Robert.

Papa was a smart man. He'd figured it out. The dowry he'd promised the Murphys was in the bank. She wasn't sure how much was actually in there, but he'd made the promise. She'd been preparing for her transition for months. He'd helped in all ways he could, letting her visit the general store more often to learn about the townspeople and teaching her to dance.

But he hadn't prepared her heart for what might sneak in.

Clay had gotten under her skin. Awakened her soul and set her body on fire.

He would be impossible to forget. No matter how the thought of settling into the life she was meant to have, without him, made her heart ache, she didn't regret a moment of it.

She was alive because of Clay. In all the ways that mattered.

It was nearly impossible to quiet her thoughts long enough to rest, but the exhaustion in her body did finally take over, and she slept.

CHAPTER 18

A pair of golden finches fluttered about on a fence post near the house. One puffed its feathers and rubbed its beak on the other, who twittered and sung a sweet song. Sadie watched them with mild interest. Although anything was better than Mary Lou's constant chatter.

"I told that woman that the blue was just not going to work for me. I wanted the teal like she had in the catalog and nothing less. I don't want some bluebell dress like everyone else is wearing, am I right?"

Robert's mother and sister Lilah sat next to her, rocking in their wooden rockers and working away on colorful knitting projects. Mary Lou, a bubbly blonde that never stopped talking, held the yarn for Mrs. Murphy's project.

"I like that blue dress," Lilah added.

"Sure, it goes well with your eyes, but I don't need to be running around in bluebell. It just doesn't go. Besides, Mrs. Smith and Carol Ann have it already. I can't be matching them, can I?" She wrinkled her nose with a snort, flashing a big smile. "Unless you think some of them Murphy boys would like it."

Sadie set the sock she was working on in her lap once more to look out over the field. Mrs. Murphy had handed her some thread and a basket of socks that needed darning when they stepped out onto the porch that morning.

Breakfast had been polite. Mr. Murphy welcomed her back before going out onto the farm to get the day started. Robert's younger brother and sister didn't speak much. Mrs. Murphy declared that she had moved up the wedding date to accommodate Sadie needing somewhere to stay.

It was not proper for her to live with them long-term otherwise, Mrs. Murphy had reminded her.

The thought of marrying Robert in just two weeks, however, made Sadie's lungs shut down. Mrs. Murphy had then turned the discussion to the approaching cold weather. The snow was moving down the mountain peaks, and the cold season would be upon them before they knew it. Despite the woman never looking in her direction, Sadie couldn't help but think the update was directed at her. To remind her that she had a broken cabin, no food reserves, and no one to help her.

Getting married could be the only thing that saved her life.

She should have been grateful that Papa had secured her before he was gone. Even if being handed the entire family's holy socks to darn and made to sit with the women on the porch was less than thrilling.

"I've seen him stare at that blue, boy, I tell you," Mary Lou said with a laugh. "I know he likes it. It'd go well with his eyes too. All you Murphys got them shiny hazel eyes."

"It does run in the family," Mrs. Murphy said. "My mama had them too. All my babies have them. I hope my grandbabies do too."

Sadie was listening just enough to catch Mrs. Murphy's glance in her direction. She pasted on a friendly smile.

Having Robert's sweet hazel-eyed babies would be a blessing, wouldn't it?

Her throat pinched close.

"I'm sure Robert will." Mary Lou's eyes were on her too. "He's so handsome. His babies will be beautiful."

"I'm sure they will," Sadie managed.

"You must be so excited! To be getting married to the eldest Murphy boy in just a fortnight." Mary Lou fanned at her face dramatically. "Pick of the litter, that one. Besides you, dear." She waved a hand at Lilah with a smile. "You can see him from a mile away walking through town. That jaw. That smile."

Mary Lou made an exaggerated saucy growl that straightened Sadie's back. She stared at the woman silently for a beat. Part of her wanted to lift a hand to the silly girl for being so forward and flirty with Robert, her declared fiancé. What did she think she was doing? The louder part of Sadie's soul, however, couldn't picture Robert's smile, even though she knew it was charming. The only one that came to mind was Clay's.

The crooked grins he gave her beneath the shadow of his hat. The way his eyes glowed when he looked at her.

Her heart skipped a beat, and her cheeks warmed. She looked out over the field once more so the other women would not see.

A movement far across the pasture caught her attention. A black hat behind the corner of the barn. Square shoulders and long legs.

Clay.

Her heart stopped, and she nearly choked, sitting straight up in her seat. The women nearby shifted. She could feel their eyes on her.

"I, er, I need to stretch my legs." Sadie slid out of her chair, dropping a couple socks onto the porch before dumping the rest of them into the basket next to her seat.

"Is everything all right?" Mrs. Murphy asked, reaching a hand out to touch her, but Sadie was already moving toward the edge of the porch.

"Of course. I just like to take a brisk walk after breakfast. It helps wake me up." Her dress shoes snapped down the wooden steps. "I felt myself falling asleep!" She threw a smile back at the women to assure them, surprised at the positive energy coursing through her veins all of a sudden.

Mary Lou called out something else, but Sadie was on the move and didn't hear her. She tried to keep her pace at a normal level, but adrenaline pulsed through her.

What was Clay doing there anyway? Despite the flicker in her chest at seeing him, it was dangerous for him to be wandering around town where he could be seen. Would someone recognize him?

Especially after robbing the mail wagon the day before. There was no doubt they were looking for suspects for that crime. Had he been reported? She hated to think of what would happen if Robert or any of his family saw Clay hiding behind their barn. What if they saw her out there with him?

Her step faltered as she considered the possibility. If she was caught she'd be in big trouble. Not to mention Mr. Murphy was a big name in town. Would they give Clay a harsher sentence for associating with her?

Among other things.

An odd shiver ran through her body as she slowed to a near stop.

She should go back. Not fan the flames.

There was the edge of Clay's hat at the corner of the barn again. He'd seen her, and he was close to exposing himself.

A new surge of frustration hit her. Didn't outlaws, of all people, know how to lay low?

She stomped through the long grass, hands clenched at her sides until she reached the barn. When she popped around the corner, Clay's hand closed over her arm and jerked her behind cover.

The furrow in his brow and the stern set in his jaw were starkly conflicting to the soft hands that moved into the hair at her neck and held her closer. Most of her anger deflated in a rush as his deep blue eyes captivated her.

"Sadie," he breathed, and the ragged sound rattled her soul.

But she was angry at him. For his indifference toward her earlier. For his indifference toward his own self-protection, coming on the farm like it was nothing.

She thrashed against him.

"What happened?" he asked, his fingers tightening on her arms. "Did someone hurt you? If someone hurt you, I'll see that they—"

"Hurt me?" She gave a haughty laugh. "You mean like this?" She shook the forearms in his strong grasp closer to his face, but he didn't let go. "You mean like back there when you said—"

His face came at her so suddenly that her lips were parted when his met hers. She jumped and twisted against the kiss, even as the shock and warmth of his touch surged through her and stirred her insides.

But no! She was still angry.

She shoved against him as he stepped into her, pushing her back against the barn wall. His chest was a strong weight across her front. Comforting in a strange way. His arms pinned her hands to the faded wooden boards on either side of her head. The thrill that shot through her, being held tight below Clay's strong body, was exciting enough that she lost track of the first reason she was mad.

He shouldn't be at the Murphy's ranch, that was for sure. She was definitely mad about that.

She pressed her mouth in harder to his so he'd truly know her frustration. She lifted up on her toes, defiantly crushing her lips to his and growling into his throat. A deep appreciative moan rattled in his chest, tickling against her and stirring a fire in the pit of her stomach.

She really couldn't think when he made noises like that.

When his tongue shot out and his pelvis moved into hers, all her thoughts grew blurry. She arched back, threading her fingers through his. He reacted in same, squeezing her hands in a firm grip. His body pressed to hers from toe to chest, and she was reminded of the weight of him, lying in her bed in the cabin. Her heart thumped, and his lips twisted against hers, eating up the tiny smile that had formed there.

The solid bulge in his pants pressed into her thigh, and the very thought of it touching her sent electricity through her limbs. She wanted to touch the sparks to him, shock some sense into him. Or set his skin on fire like hers.

When his grip on her loosened, her hands slid up his arms, over his solid body, and down his waist to dig her fingers under the belt on either side of his hips. She took a firm hold and hauled him closer to her, grinding his hips into her body.

Clay's hot mouth moved over her jaw and down her neck, nipping and sucking at her skin. Her eyes rolled as she tilted her head back against the wall, allowing him more access to her throat. The heat from his lips and breath were like fire, scorching her flesh, and it stirred her so deep down that her pulse tripped. She jerked his hips again, and her breath shuttered as his erection stabbed into her legs, a solid nudge in between her thighs. Her body burned to feel more of him, and she grew desperate.

Her hands slid along around to the front of his belt,

disarming the belt buckle with fumbling fingers. As she made quick work of his trouser fastenings, he moaned into her mouth. The flame within her raged, and she wrapped a leg around him as she pushed his pants open and freed the thick length of him.

He growled into her lips, jerking her skirts up out of the grass and shoving them up over her hips. With one smooth motion, he slid his hands down around her rear and hoisted her up the wall.

Her fingers wrapped around his shaft, sliding from tip to base, and he hissed a breath against her mouth. One of his hands moved from her bottom to her thighs, ripping her undergarments away.

She gasped, panting in surprise as his fingers slid along the sensitive folds beneath. Then his hand was supporting her once more, lifting her higher, and fitting her over his hips. She snatched her hands away, wrapping her legs around his waist and drawing him in closer with a jerk. When the length of him delved deep, her breath caught, a jolt of excitement coursing through her.

She'd ached to have him again for what felt like a lifetime. Two days was much too long to go without having him close enough to smell, to taste, to feel lodged between her thighs.

The delicious sensation that leapt up from the junction between her legs and through her abdomen intoxicated her. Her fingers threaded through his hair, tightening and pulling him nearer. His teeth sank into her lip, testing and teasing. She moaned.

His hips pulled away from hers and returned with even greater force, crushing her against the barn wall. She cried out, but his mouth muffled the sound. His hips jerked, forcing him deeper and deeper. Long, rough strokes that pounded her into the wood.

The hot core he hammered with his body roared, liquid

fire tightening low in her abdomen like an explosive knot. Her legs clenched around him, fingers clawing through his hair and into his scalp as she demanded more of him.

He delivered. Faster and harder rolls of his hips, bruising lips on hers. She nearly couldn't catch her breath in the fervor.

When she thought she might suffocate, or her body explode, his tightened. He hit her even deeper in her center, and she erupted. She gasped into his mouth, and he groaned. A hot wave of ecstasy rocked her as his body seized along with her.

Her body was on fire, and it took a few moments for the waves of heat to subside.

He tucked his face into the hollow of her neck. The sound of his quivering breaths in her ear was as tempting as the rest of his body.

They stood in silence, locked against the barn wall. As their breaths began to settle, his hands grew soft on her. He lifted her from his body and set her feet back on the grass. When she was grounded once more, a new heat filled her cheeks.

What the hell had she just done?

She chanced a peek up at him as she set her skirts straight. His gaze was on her as he fixed his pants. His eyes shone brightly, lips pink and puffy where they'd used them so roughly. A part of her wanted to run her tongue along her lips to get another taste of him. The other was appalled as reality set in.

She'd come out to set him straight, and he'd bewitched her.

But she'd be lying if she said it hadn't been amazing.

She swallowed roughly, digging down deep to find what she'd come out to say.

Only he spoke first.

"Come back with me, Sadie."

It snapped her back. The truth. Everything that'd happened before she arrived at the Murphy ranch.

She put her hands on her hips with a sharp frown.

"So you can sell me away to a witch?"

CHAPTER 19

Clay's brow deepened, and he narrowed his eyes. "What are you talking about?"

Sadie dug into the side pocket of her now-wrinkled green cotton dress and pulled out a creased piece of paper. She snatched it open and shoved it toward him.

"She doesn't want me. You aren't going to get any money," she said, swallowing back a stream of tears. She refused to cry in front of him over such a matter.

She wasn't sure why she'd read Aunt Hilda's letter again half a dozen times, but the sting had rung true each time.

Clay's eyes scanned the page quickly, then jumped up to her.

"This is your aunt?"

Sadie gave him a tight-lipped nod.

His mouth curled in a snarl, and he ripped the letter in two. It jolted her like a slap in the face. Stiff and wide-eyed, she stared at him as the leaflets floated into the grass at their feet.

"Hang what she says," he grunted. "Who cares if she won't pay anything?"

"You do apparently. You were going to drag me over there."

He scoffed with a shake of his head. "Ace wanted me to go collect. I was just doing as he asked. I actually wasn't going to mention it to you." His voice lowered, and his eyes softened. "After I brought you back to camp, I was going to tell Ace I wanted to keep you around for a bit. I mean, you know, you didn't really have a good place to go back to. Bears and all. I thought maybe you'd stick around..."

His eyes pulled her, and she wanted to step back into his arms. To be enveloped against his chest. If only he wasn't so reckless. Putting his life on the line for Ace and constantly doing his bidding. She needed a more stable life. Like living on a ranch.

His eyes sharpened.

"But I got caught up," he said, "and I forgot about women and their reputations. Worrying so much about what everyone else thinks of you. It controls your life. It changes who you are. I didn't expect you to walk down the street on my arm or nothing, but you dumped me like breakfast scraps in the pig trough."

The pain and frustration in his eyes sliced into her heart. She shook her head, reaching out for his arm, but he moved it just out of reach.

"I'm sorry," she sputtered. "I didn't mean to hurt you. It's just that Mr. Brown knows everything in town. He and the rest of Emerald Falls know I'm engaged to Robert. I wasn't sure what he'd—"

"Are you still?"

She blinked. "Am I what?"

"Are you still engaged?" Clay took hold of her elbow, staring down at her in earnest from the shadows of his hat. "Do you love him?"

She wanted to shrink into her body and run. She'd never

felt so trapped in her entire life, staring up into the glowing blue eyes. They were strong, fixed on her, waiting for a response, but her breath was gone. Her thoughts galloping across her brain in wild abandonment.

She had no answer for him.

She'd wanted to love Robert, and she'd always believed that one day she would.

But her body burned for Clay.

Even his fingers on her arm scorched into her skin. Her cheeks warmed, and her body came to attention. She couldn't keep the image of his half-naked body from her mind. The feeling of his naked flesh on hers. The wooden wall biting into her back as he ravished her front. The way his body had moved against hers in the darkness of the cabin, a beautiful harmony that had left her breathless and alive. The way he'd taken her roughly there in the field. It all was so vivid in her mind that she could hardly formulate other thoughts.

But he was an outlaw. He put himself in dangerous situations that would get him killed. She'd already lost the most important man in her life. She couldn't stomach it happening again. Not with Clay.

Besides, Papa had chosen Robert for her, and she trusted his judgment. He'd been her rock for her entire life, and she'd only just met Clay. How could she just dump Papa's opinion like it meant nothing? She knew he had her best interest at heart when he'd arranged the marriage, and it was a good fit. A smart fit.

If only Robert spoke to her soul the way Clay did. Sparked her curiosity and breathed life into her body.

But her life had been figured out long before Clay arrived. Who was she to spoil that?

Her teeth sunk into her lower lip as her body quaked, weakening under Clay's gaze. His fingers tightened on her arm, and she was afraid if she didn't give the right answer, he wouldn't let her go. She wasn't sure she'd be strong enough to fight him off when all she wanted to do was fold into him.

So she lied.

"Of course I love him."

The way his face fell split her heart in two. His eyes were empty again, and she knew it was her only chance to run.

She pulled her arm away, and he let it go. She fell back a few steps along the wall, ready to flee.

"You are so stubborn."

His words snapped into her like a whip. He pulled back, crossing his arms over his chest, and regarded her with a hard face.

"I know you want to honor your father's wishes and make him happy, but, Sadie, your father's dead. You don't have to make him happy anymore."

She gaped at him, feeling her chest crack open a little more.

"Besides," he continued, "your parents don't always know best. I should know. You remember I told you my mother left me behind with her aunt? Ma picked up a drinking problem after my father left. She wasn't a particularly stable woman, so she handed us over. Her aunt tried to raise Tom and me up, but she didn't have a clue how to love children. She tried, I think, but she was clueless.

"Though she seemed like a saint next to her husband. He didn't care who he hurt. He liked ropes and belts, and sometimes wooden boards. Liked to beat us around on a daily basis. He broke my arm once. That's when Tom stood up for me. He picked fights just to steer the asshole off me. Damn ol' Uncle Roy really tanned his hide too. I could hear Tom crying himself to sleep some nights.

"There was no one to turn to and nowhere to go. I'd have

much rather stayed with our mother, no matter how ill-suited she thought she was. At least she would have loved us."

Sadie's dry throat throbbed as tears knotted there, threatening to burst loose.

"Oh, Clay," she whispered.

Her heart lurched. She wanted to throw her arms around him, but he stayed a safe distance away.

"The point is," he said, "in the end, you just have to ask yourself which is more important. Doing what he thought was right, or accepting where love truly lies?"

She stumbled back with a hand on her chest. Clay's eyes were on fire, and the tendon in his jaw flexed. The large chest beneath the parted edges of his shirt collar rose high and fell as the frustration boiled within him. She was afraid it might burst out. He was a beast.

And he loved her.

Her own frustrations slammed through her. Love, passion, fear, anger. She clenched her fists at her side, digging her toes into the grass.

"Love won't save you, Clay. I could love you to the moon and back, and it won't protect you."

His brow furrowed, and he shook his head. "What are you talking about?"

"This life you have!" She gaped. "The shooting and the stealing."

"We try not to—"

"I know, you go the peaceful route, but that's when you can. What was that yesterday? With the coach? I thought that was supposed to be a quick, easy thing. You could have died!"

Some of the sharp edges in his face eased as he rubbed fingers over his rough chin. If she wasn't mistaken, Clay Pearson looked almost sheepish. Caught in the act.

"All the love I possessed didn't save my father, Clay. It

won't save you either." Tears trickled from the corners of her eyes, and she let them.

He lifted hands, opening his mouth, but seemed at a loss for words. She ground her foot into the grass and kept going.

"Now I'm sorry your mother made an ill decision, but I value my father's opinion. He was a smart and caring man." Tears choked her words. "He wouldn't have led me astray. I've been listening to his advice decades longer than I've known you."

Clay pressed his lips into a firm line.

"That's fine. I get that. It's nice to have something to believe in. Although, I gotta say, I believe your father would have made a different decision." He rolled his shoulders back as he took a step away.

She frowned, an edge of curiosity moving her forward a step, but Clay spoke over her.

"By the way, I found out your father's secret. I knew he had one."

His back turned as he edged away. She rocked off her feet to leap after him, but he turned back to look at her over his shoulder.

"Those letters under his bed I told you to read? I assume you haven't. Some were between him and your aunt. She was so angry at him for running off with your mother, taking on a poor widow and her little girl."

Sadie frowned as the words swam in her head. They didn't make sense. She tried to grasp them and put them into the puzzle of the past she knew, but they wouldn't fit.

"What?"

"That's your father's secret. Or at least Jed Tanner's. He's not your father."

The ground fell out from under her, and she nearly toppled to her knees.

"That's a lie," she stammered.

"It's not. Go read the letters."

A new fire flamed inside her. "I don't need to read the letters. I know the truth, and I know what I need to do. You should just get on back to Ace. Pick up some more orders to follow."

The rim of his hat nearly touched his shoulder as he peered back at her from the shadows. "I don't need any new orders. I'm on some. To bring you back. But don't worry, you won't see me again. Go enjoy your new happy."

Then he walked across the field without looking back.

CHAPTER 20

Sadie's knife rocked back and forth over the wooden cutting block as she sliced a carrot. When she reached the end, she used the blade to swipe the chunks into a large pile she'd created. Then she set the knife aside and wiped her hands on her apron.

"She had no idea what'd hit her, the poor girl," Mrs. Murphy laughed as she rinsed peeled potatoes in the sink. "First she was standing quietly in the stall, waiting to be milked, and the next she was nearly climbing out the other side, trying to get away from sticky little Robert."

Lilah snickered, and Sadie hummed a small laugh to humor the woman.

Mrs. Murphy had been going on and on about her precious first born for the last hour, her latest story involving a young Robert smacking cattle on the rear end with honey-covered fingers to watch the insects swarm around. It sounded disgusting and cruel to her, but she wasn't in the mood to cross the oddly proud mother.

Lilah stirred a large bowl of dough, barely making a sound. Sadie'd tried to have a normal conversation about life on the ranch with her earlier, but Lilah had made it difficult, only answering in short answers and refraining from speaking all together when she could.

Sadie gathered the chopped carrots and dumped them into a bowl on the counter next to a quarter cut of a skinned hog. One of Mr. Murphy's men had come in a few moments before, slapped the meat onto the counter unceremoniously, and left. Sadie looked it over as she picked her knife up again.

"Do you want me to cut the pork chops and backstrap out of this?" she asked.

Mrs. Murphy looked up at her with a subtle tilt of her brow. "You know how to cut those?"

Sadie rolled the knife stock in her palm as she regarded the older woman. "Sure. I used to cut our meat back home."

The left side of Mrs. Murphy's face bunched in a horrified grimace. "Your father let you butcher the meat?"

Sadie paused alongside the hog and lowered the knife. She hadn't expected the sound of horror in the woman's voice. She considered backtracking and saying she'd misunderstood the question, but the conversation had been quite basic. She'd never get away with that fib. An uncomfortable heat itched into the edges of her ears and cheekbones.

"Sometimes he did."

Mrs. Murphy shuddered, pressing a wet finger to her temple. "My gracious, you poor girl. Next, you'll tell me he took you hunting as well."

Metal clattered on the counter. Sadie cleared her throat as she gathered her dropped knife without a word. Mrs. Murphy craned her head to stare.

"Heavenly stars, you must be joking. How barbaric. What on earth was your father thinking?"

Sadie bit into the side of her cheek to keep from snapping

back. Helping Papa with his business when he was all on his own was not barbaric. She'd been proud to help him.

"He needed the help. It was just the two of us after all," she said.

Mrs. Murphy stacked the potatoes on the counter with a shake of her head. "Horrible. No little girl should go through that. Don't worry, you won't do anything like that here. You won't have the time for it."

"Hunting," Lilah snorted under her breath, an amused smirk on her face.

Sadie pursed her lips in frustration and hid behind the honey-colored veil of her hair as she washed her knife in the sink basin.

Once the potatoes were arranged on the counter, Mrs. Murphy wiped her hands on her apron and gave Sadie a tight smile.

"You'll learn to help Robert on the ranch. There's a large staff and plenty of paperwork to handle. Not to mention cooking and patching clothes. Once all those babies come along, your hands will be full, my dear. You can leave the hunting to the men."

The woman started slicing the potatoes with a smug smile, while Sadie stared at the counter until her eyes glazed over.

She could see herself, stuck in one of the rocking chairs on the porch, a small mountain of socks to darn and patches to sew stacked next to her. Screaming children that looked oddly like what she'd imagined sticky-fingered Robert looked like ran about, while their father sat at a table reading a newspaper.

"Brown is getting those square-toed boots I like in black," he might say with a hearty chuckle. "Brilliant. I'll have to pop over there this afternoon."

Sadie nearly couldn't contain her eye-roll.

Such silly petty things he worried about. Was his entire life that way? What of the people in it?

Her stomach soured, and she grimaced.

As if called from the recesses of her brain, a flash of memory jumped at her. Riding horses along the river's edge with Clay. The excitement of the wind streaming through her hair and clinging to the galloping mare as she leapt through the air. The wild abandonment in Clay's eyes as he pinned her to the tree and kissed her like it was the most natural thing in the world.

She longed for that excitement again.

Surely Robert had some excitement in him somewhere.

Her memory was shattered when boots came stomping up the front steps and into the kitchen.

"Speak of the devil," Mrs. Murphy cooed, and Sadie's heart sank. "How are my boys this afternoon?"

Robert and his brother Nathan hovered in the doorway.

"Afternoon, Mama," Nathan said, then gave an appreciative sniff. "I smell cornbread."

"You know you do, dear."

He grinned, the same charming look Robert had. It was a wonder he was so close to marrying age and still without a candidate.

"You ladies cooking?" Robert asked as he stepped near Sadie.

"Almost," she said. "Prepping. I suppose we have a long way to go."

"I'm teaching her the Texas Strawback Roast you love so much." Mrs. Murphy gave Robert a wink.

"Perfect," he said with a grin. "Any wife of mine certainly needs to know that one."

Sadie's lips quirked in a small smile, even if she wasn't thrilled by the notion of memorizing all his mother's recipes.

"We'll leave you busy ladies to it then. We just need this

chest of branding irons," Robert said as he stepped up to a large wooden box tucked into the corner.

"Good. Get that thing out of my kitchen," Mrs. Murphy said. "Your father dropped it in here this morning, and it's been in the way."

Robert stooped down to take hold of the side handles and pulled back with a low grunt. The box shifted but didn't lift. His face flushed, and he let go to rub a hand over it.

"Nate, give me a hand, would you?"

His brother moved up alongside him and helped him haul the chest into the air. Nathan shouldered most of the weight, and Sadie wondered if he could have picked it up on his own. Robert had made it look impossible.

The scene made her stomach quiver and feel a bit ill, though she couldn't pinpoint entirely why. Something about it brought back the afternoon they'd been cornered by the wolf. The way Robert had backed her away and refused to let her grab her gun. He'd glared at her when she'd done it anyway, and never given her any proper appreciation for saving his behind when the wolf lunged at him.

"I hope dinner will be ready soon," Robert said as the men hauled the trunk out the door.

"Get Jim to come cut this meat," Mrs. Murphy said, waving a rag in their direction.

When the men were gone, she gave Sadie a pointed look as she washed her hands. "Jim can take care of that thing. We have enough to worry about."

Sadie helped her with vegetables and Lilah with the breads before being dismissed. She had enough time before dinner to wash up and stand at the window in her bedroom, staring out at the horses grazing in the pasture down the field. They were bathed in the pink glow of the setting sun, but she could still make out Clover's silhouette.

The horse she'd ridden in on but didn't actually own. She

really should return her to the Van den Bergs, but making a trip back there wasn't something she was sure she could stomach. Going back out there, to the peaceful campsite away from town, full of close-knit family and friends. Looking back on her stay there, it'd been an enjoyable one. She'd been a captive to begin with, but after the first night, it'd been easy to forget.

She'd never felt unwelcome.

She'd even made some friends.

The thought of the smiling faces she'd left made her feel hollow and alone.

Clara, Ginny, Bridget, Mason.

Clay.

She took a long breath as she looked away from the gray mare and went back out to eat.

Dinner was another long, drawn-out conversation about cattle and politics with the men. She didn't even attempt to speak, just nibbled on the food she'd worked so hard to put on the table, and excused herself early.

Back in her bedroom she sat on the edge of the bed and put her face in her hands. Would the rest of her life be made up of working in the kitchen with her mother-in-law, who was disgusted by her past and didn't trust her as far as she could throw her, and listening to the men speak freely while she was to sit in silence as a proper woman should? All for what, to appease the weak man whose touch did not stir her?

She cursed herself for allowing Clay to touch her. She was ruined. She'd never have known a man could set her skin on fire had he not come along.

And yet. She dragged her fingers down her cheeks and choked back the tears that stung her eyes. She still did not regret meeting Clay. Falling for him. Allowing herself to be happy with him.

If only Papa had met him.

The thought stirred her, and she recalled Clay's words.

Jed Tanner was not her father.

She'd gone back to a hundred times, of course, but she'd built up a solid assurance in herself that it was a lie. Of course he was her father. He'd been Mama's husband when she was born. He'd raised her after Mama was gone. There'd never been any indication she should question it.

Except for Clay's words.

Her teeth pinched her lip as she looked at her small stack of belongings on the stool by the bed. The items from her saddlebags, the last of everything she owned. Among them was the stack of letters Clay had given her.

She stared at them for a long ragged breath before she retrieved them. Spread out on the bed there seemed to be a hundred of them. Folded white pages, some faded and crinkled. She picked up the closest one to her and read the first few lines.

Dearest Jed,

Do return home soon. Your father misses you so. I know you are looking for your future, and we are pleased, but he has been sour this last month without you.

Sadie skimmed the unfamiliar handwriting to the name at the bottom. Beatrice Tanner. Papa's mother.

She picked up another.

My idiot brother Jed,

You cannot possibly be serious. Mother and Father got your wedding announcement today. To say they are surprised is nothing. I think Father broke his favorite cigar box. You know, that one we're not supposed to touch? What have you done?

We're all happy you've found someone to love, but you know you can't marry her. It's one thing to pick up a pretty girl while you're looking to make a new life, but marrying the first one you find and taking on her problems? I thought you were smarter than that.

Let that girl and her baby be and come on home, Jed.

Sadie's heart flopped, and she gripped the page tighter.

There's no reason to be so stubborn. You know Father will cut you off. What will you do for money?

Hope to see you soon,

Hilda Tanner

Sadie dropped the letter on the bed while her heart raced.

It was true. Papa had met Mama when she already had a baby.

Sadie's face flushed, and she tugged at the neck of her dress. How had she never known? Why had they lied?

She frowned, digging for another letter and finding familiar masculine handwriting.

My dear Eleanor,

Sadie's back straightened. Mama. She put all her effort into not crinkling the page with her clenched fingers.

I am more convinced of my love for you than ever. I miss your beautiful eyes and the soft pink of your cheeks. I will not sleep properly until I can kiss you goodnight.

I am sorry I had to leave on short notice, but it was my worst fear as suspected. My father has been diagnosed with pneumonia. The doctor does not have much positive to say on his recovery.

I am going to have a difficult time getting home, as my family have turned into raving monsters. I don't understand why they feel so strongly that I should move back to St. Aspen, but none of their words will work on me. I know they haven't met you and Sadie yet, but they will fall in love as fast as I did, I'm sure. Who could resist your charm, and Sadie's sweet blonde curls? I have no doubts, even if they are a pain right now. Hopefully, I can coerce them into better moods so they will attend the wedding ceremony next month.

I will be on the first train back to Emerald Falls in the morning. I count the breaths until I see your face again, my love. You keep my heart beating as I dream of you.

Forever yours,

Jed Tanner

Sadie closed her eyes and pressed the sheet of paper against her chest.

Even as a young child, she'd never doubted her parents love for one another. Reading the actual words brought fresh tears to her eyes. They stung, and she welcomed them.

She missed Mama and Papa both. Even if she had learned more truth than she cared to know. Jed Tanner was still her father in her heart. In the ten years he'd raised her on his own, she'd never doubted him. She still didn't.

Except perhaps his choice in men.

If only he'd met Clay.

Especially after reading of Papa's stubborn attachment to love, she felt assured he would have picked Clay.

Perhaps she'd made a mistake denying her heart.

Clay was right. Papa would have made the other decision. He'd have picked love.

The thought brought a fresh wave of tears, and she curled up among Papa's letters and cried herself to sleep.

CHAPTER 21

Sadie twirled her silver fork through a nest of yellow and green vegetables and sighed. Robert's grandfather and Mr. Murphy had been discussing their different approaches to branding cattle for the last twenty minutes of lunch. She'd never been so disinterested in the ranching business in her life. If she'd ever romanticized what it would be like to be married to a rancher, the vision was gone.

The Murphy approach to ranching was dry.

"You just snag those calves by the ears and give 'em a squeeze," Grandpa said. "Then you stick that iron on while it's good and hot."

"If you make them squeal, though, those mamas will come after you," Mr. Murphy said.

Grandpa huffed out a dismissive breath. "Not if you put those girls out in the back forty. Ain't no way they're getting back to those babies."

"I prefer the cleaner method. Tie the hock, do it quick."

"That's how you get kicked in the head."

Mr. Murphy grunted.

"That's fine, Grandpa," Robert said, "but how do you keep up with the numbers is the real question. There's no way to properly count them all each time you move them. There's thousands in that sea of black out there. How do you know how many you leave with?"

Sadie rolled her eyes, pushing the food on her plate and doing her best to avoid propping her chin in her hand and taking a snooze.

"Divide 'em up. Count in sections. Same way we been doing it for generations. You can count, can'tcha, boy?"

"Of course, but that takes a lot of time."

"For the cowboys. That's their job."

"Couldn't you just give them different brands or colors?" Sadie asked, attempting to dip a toe into the conversation to keep herself awake.

Mrs. Murphy narrowed her eyes from across the table and cleared her throat. "Let the men talk their business," she hissed in a hushed tone.

Sadie pressed her lips together in frustration, biting back a retort.

Let them talk? They'd been going on and on about ridiculous matters for ages, and no one else was allowed to speak?

She set her fork aside and leaned back in her chair, staring out a nearby window. White clouds dotted a soft blue sky. A flock of birds cut through them.

To be flying free in the sky, far away from the boring life she'd been dropped into, sounded like a dream. The perfect solution to the walls that were closing in. A sigh slipped out of her lips.

Something touched her leg, and she jumped. Robert's fingers hovered near her knee. While Grandpa and Mr. Murphy continued to debate around them, he looked at her with a small smile as his hand rested over hers on her thigh. Her muscles tensed.

His skin was cool against hers, and she dug her fingertips into her dress to fight the urge to yank her hand free. His clammy palm brought no spark, no fire. Just tension and a queasy feeling in her gut.

Was this the touch she would have to endure for the rest of her life?

Knowing what a truly passionate touch felt like?

She squirmed in her seat, looking out the window again. Another pair of birds sailed through the endless blue. Free and alive.

Suddenly words from Papa's letters came rushing in.

I am more convinced of my love for you than ever.

Why was she fighting her feelings with such conviction? Papa hadn't done it. He'd left everything he knew to follow Mama.

Deep down inside, she felt that if Papa had met Clay, he would have picked him a hundred times over Robert.

The realization of all her true feelings hit her like a freight train.

She'd made a big mistake.

But she was determined to fix that.

Clay may have let her escape, but he still held her heart captive.

When Robert's fingers squeezed into hers, Sadie jolted alert and snatched her hand away. Her chair nearly toppled as she pushed back from the table and leapt to her feet.

All of the family seated around her stopped and stared, frozen in confusion. Robert sat still, a puzzled look deepening into an annoyed frown on his face.

"Oh, excuse me," she stammered. Her brain raced faster than her mouth could formulate actual words. "I need to take a walk."

As she hurried around the head of the table, all gazes followed her.

Robert stood abruptly. “Sadie. What’s going on?”

“I’ll just be a moment,” she coughed, letting the lie sting her tongue. It didn’t matter. She’d soon be free.

Heavy boots echoed on the wood floor as he came around the table after her. Then his hand was on her elbow.

“Where are you going?”

“Outside. I won’t be long.” She kept her gaze down, refusing to let him see the truth in her eyes. She wouldn’t let him stop her.

“Don’t you think it’s rude to go wandering outside while we’re eating lunch?” Robert asked, a hiss slipping out between his teeth. His fingers pinched into her arm, and her face snapped up to meet his.

His eyes were sharp, mouth set. For an instant, she was frightened. Afraid that he might prevent her from leaving. That he'd find out her secret.

But there was nothing he could do to stop her. Unless he planned on having her tied up like a dog for the rest of her life, she was going to walk away.

“I thought it’d be more rude to pass water here on the dining room floor.”

Behind Robert’s back, Mrs. Murphy threw her hand over her mouth with a gasp.

Sadie’s eyes hardened, and she snatched her arm free. “So if you’ll excuse me.”

Robert didn’t make to grab her again, but his eyes cut into her. His thin lips pressed against one another until they whitened, and she grimaced, wheeling away from him and hurrying down the hallway.

She held her breath as her dress shoes clicked on the wood, listening for the boots on her tail, but none came. She picked up the pace, passing the back door that led to the outhouse and continued down the next hallway to the bedrooms.

She had less than a minute, she figured, before someone realized she hadn't gone outside. Just enough time to snatch a few things from her room and run.

The door crashed open under her hand, and she dove for the saddle bag in the corner. She'd brought it in from the barn a few days ago to store her things. Thank goodness. Perhaps she'd known all along, deep down in the depths of her soul, that she couldn't stay. Her destiny lay elsewhere.

She double-checked the side stuffed with letters. They were bundled neatly inside, all read at least once by now. She smiled at the sight of them and buckled the flap back. Then she ripped a couple dresses from the stool next to her bed and shoved them down in the second satchel. The pants and shirt she'd arrived in had since disappeared, but she hadn't been shocked by it. Thankfully it was no longer his business what she wore.

Her boots still sat in the corner, however, and she kicked off her dress shoes to pull them on. They peered out from beneath the hem of her long olive green dress.

Then she was gone.

She crept back down the hall in a rush. Her boots made less noise than the hard soles of those heeled shoes, but she still didn't want to draw attention. At the rear exit, she slipped outside silently and closed the door.

The wind and fresh air hit her like a wave of euphoria.

It'd never occurred to her how trapped she'd been living in the forest with Papa. Sure, she was outside and away from all the busy town, but she was still confined to the cabin or anywhere she traveled with Papa. She'd never felt so free as she had riding next to Clay in the forest or sitting around the campfire with the Van den Berg women. She had people to talk to and new things to see.

Coming back to the Murphy plantation had opened her

eyes. It was worse than her small cabin in the woods. Even with people bustling around it all the time, it was lonely.

With her saddlebags hoisted on her shoulder, Sadie ran for the barn. Her dress gathered and flowed around her legs in the tall grass. Even with the sun at high noon, the air had a chill. It was energizing, and she grinned as she ran.

One of the wide barn doors stood open, and she dashed inside and down the aisle. Clover stood dozing in a stall near the front, and her ears perked up at the approaching footsteps.

"Hey, shh. It's me," Sadie whispered.

She dropped the satchels and opened the stall. The mare whuffled a greeting as Sadie led her out.

"Be quiet. We're getting out of here."

The saddle she'd ridden in on was propped next to the wall. Her short frame was almost too small to get the saddle up over her shoulder, but she flung it with a surprising burst of energy. She secured her tack and saddlebags with excited fingers, then mounted in a flurry.

"Let's get out of here!" she whispered.

Clover clopped down the barn aisle and out the open door. Her muscles bunched to take off across the grass, but she jolted to the side with a sheer whinny instead. Sadie grabbed a fistful of her mane to keep from toppling off and held tight as the horse tossed her head. When Sadie managed to pull herself upright, she saw what had spooked her.

Robert was crouched just outside the door, arms up to shield his face from the excited horse. His eyes met hers, and he popped up again, lowering his hands to smooth out his vest.

"What is going on?" he barked.

She considered telling him for half a breath, but the very thought of discussing it with him turned her stomach. She didn't want a single other person to tell her what was best for her.

After a short pause, she pulled on Clover's reins and wheeled her around the side of the barn. Robert shouted after them, but Sadie didn't look back. She just leaned over the mare's shoulders and asked her for more speed. They flew across the field.

People were yelling back at the house. Sadie peeked under her elbow. The family was standing outside, watching the chaos. Mrs. Murphy was marching toward Robert and the barn, pointing and yelling.

"That's your capital! Don't let her get away!"

Sadie squeezed her knees in tighter to Clover's side and set her eyes on the road ahead. Her freedom.

The Murphy plantation sat just on the edge of Emerald Falls, less than a mile from the main street, and as soon as she rode out from beyond the buildings and onto the road, she could see the town in the distance. Her heart sang. Soon she would be away from the Murphys and on her way back to Clay.

Except she didn't know where the Van den Berg camp was.

Only that it was on the opposite side of Emerald Falls. Once she was through town, she could try to pinpoint where in the trees it might be. There were only so many forests in the Absaroka Valley. She just had to keep pressing forward.

It didn't take them long to reach town at a full gallop, but they had to drop their pace quickly once they arrived.

Emerald Falls was a busy place at noon. Pedestrians were everywhere. Even groups of children out to play during lunch time ran up and down the main street. A handful of wagons moved along either side of the pathway with horse and riders meandering through.

It was a rare sight for Sadie, who normally helped Papa

sell his wares in the early morning and saw little of the actual life around Emerald Falls. She stared for a moment before setting her eyes on the post office at the far end of the long strip. That was her way out. Beyond the building and the train track and out into the open world.

She just had to hold onto the hope that she could navigate the big wilderness on her own.

Just as the fleeting fear passed through her, she caught a glimpse of something that nearly made her heart jump out of her body.

A cream horse's hide and the soft black and white edges of a tail disappearing around the corner of the saloon. Georgene. Excitement leapt within her like live crickets, and she could barely move her legs to push Clover on faster.

"Excuse me," Sadie murmured to no one in particular as she wove through two wagons in the road, eyes fixed on the spot she'd seen the tail disappear.

It was four buildings away, but she could make it before Georgene got too far away.

There was no way Clay would have let anyone else ride Georgene. He was in Emerald Falls. So close to her. Her fingers trembled, and her pulse thrummed through her with wild abandon.

The wagons passed and a clear strip opened on the road. Sadie heeled Clover onward, but someone stepped into their path. The mare jerked to a stop, nearly sending Sadie flying over her head. Sadie clutched at her saddle horn with a gnarled frown.

"What the hell do you—" Sadie growled and was shocked to find Mary Lou standing in the street in front of her.

The woman wore an oblivious smile, unconcerned that she'd nearly been trampled. She waved with a lighthearted greeting.

"Where you off to so fast?" the woman chirped.

Sadie weighed her options for departure. A wagon to the left. Another rider to the right, too close beyond Mary Lou to push past.

"Excuse me," Sadie scoffed, finally staring down at Mary Lou.

She didn't seem fazed by the attitude.

"You going off somewhere on your own?"

Fire boiled in Sadie's stomach. "I can go somewhere by myself if I damn well want to!"

Mary Lou's eyes widened a fraction, and she placed a hand on her chest. "My. Testy, aren't we? Why didn't you ride in with Robert?"

Sadie's fingers tightened on her reins until she thought she might rip the leather in two. "Because I didn't want to," she hissed through clenched teeth.

"Oh, I see. Did he know that? Because he's coming."

Sadie twisted in the saddle with wide eyes. At the back end of the main street, Robert pushed his black horse through stalled wagons and a group of pedestrians. His eyes locked on hers, and her soul sank with a frustrated scream.

CHAPTER 22

Sadie was kicking her horse before she was even settled back into the saddle. Clover moved her head side to side with a frustrated bellow as she tried to step past Mary Lou. The infuriating woman stood still in the road, staring up at them like a damn judgment-wielding imp.

"Move your ass!" Sadie growled as she pushed Clover forward, clipping Mary Lou in the shoulder and bouncing off the nearby horse and rider.

Sadie mumbled her apologies but kept going, finally freeing them from the tangle and trotting down the street. Pedestrians hopped to the side and hugged the edges of the road as she came through. She imagined they might all be staring at her in horror, yelling at her to slow down, but she didn't take a moment to peek at any of them. Her eyes were locked onto the red wood corner of the saloon where Georgene's tail had disappeared. Her focus sharpened still as they slowed down to make the turn.

She could not let Clay get away.

The side road traveled alongside the post office and the train track, then curved back around up through the backside of town. Beyond the edge of the mail delivery shed, wide open green fields stretched. In the distance, she spotted Georgene's flashy tail and a familiar black hat. The surge within her was enough to make her squeak out a breath.

"Go!" she breathed, setting Clover off at a gallop once more.

They thundered across the soft dirt outside the post office, passing a mail delivery coach much like the one she'd watched the Van den Bergs rob days ago, and across the train tracks. Once in the wide stretch of grass, Sadie gave the mare enough rein to open out and run at full speed.

She had no idea what she'd say to Clay once she reached him. An apology didn't seem like enough. The thought of telling him he was right stung a little, but it was true. He had been right about what she wanted, about what she needed. She didn't need to become a rancher's wife, a slave to the plantation and following Robert's orders. She needed a man who could take care of her and wouldn't be angry if she took care of herself.

She could tell him all these things, but what she really wanted to do was throw herself into his arms. She wanted that fiery touch on her skin and his mouth on hers, claiming her the way he had in the cabin. And outside the barn. Nothing had prepared her for that, and nothing would ever come close to comparing to it again.

There was no room for cold clammy hands and touches with no spark in her life. Not when there was a man that could give her everything she needed.

Her cheeks warmed, and a smile spread over her face as she stared at Clay's nearing form. She was almost close enough to yell out at him. To beg him to stop and listen.

Except they were not alone.

Another movement caught her eye.

Two other men were riding in from the west road, horses pointed at a diagonal to slide into Clay's path.

The men were dressed in dark duster coats and black hats. They gestured to each other, pointing in Clay's direction. For a moment Sadie thought they might be other Van den Bergs. Had the three of them been in Emerald Falls for another heist? More chaos? Then one of the men lifted a revolver to arm's length and aimed at Clay.

Croakers.

Sadie's lungs seized up like crystal.

They were going to kill Clay. Her brain was lost in a moment of panic before she set her jaw.

She heeled Clover hard in the flank, and they flew forward. Sadie coaxed their direction away from Clay and into the approaching Croakers.

She had no plan, but there was no way she was going to let them shoot Clay. As they neared the men, she lifted up in her saddle enough to get a good glimpse at her outlaw. He was still riding for the forest without a look back. She shouted his name.

The Croakers looked over at her, but she was already upon them. She pulled back on the reins with all her might, spinning Clover around, and they slid into the nearest Croaker. The mare's hefty hindquarters barrelled into the Croaker horse. Both he and the animal went flying, and the four of them crashed to the ground.

The impact catapulted her over Clover's shoulder and into the grass and rocks below. The ground slammed against her, knocking the air from her lungs.

Clear blue sky stretched over her for miles. The bright sun pierced her eyes.

Her chest hurt.

She needed air. Sadie arched her back and opened her

lungs, finally drawing in a fresh breath. It set her brain back on track, and she recalled her predicament.

Clay!

Scrambling around to her stomach and up to her knees, she looked around. Clover was sitting on her haunches, head lowered and sides heaving. She looked tired but not seriously injured. Near her the Croaker she'd collided with lay in a heap on the ground next to his stretched out black horse. The beast was breathing, but he wasn't making an attempt to get up.

Sadie got to her feet, dusting dirt and debris from her dress while looking for the other gunman. She heard the thundering of his horse's hooves before she turned to see him coming at her. The scowl on his bearded face was enough to turn her blood to ice. He gave a war cry as he lifted his gun in her direction, and she ducked down, scouring the ground around her for a rock or something to throw.

The end was near. She was without a weapon or a horse. She'd either be shot or trampled. She steeled her nerves, glancing down for just an instant and snatching up a jagged-edge rock. When she looked back up, she didn't even get a chance to throw before the gunshot.

She gasped, her entire body frozen in shock as the Croaker's hat popped off and went flying. He frowned and looked around with a twitch in his eye. Several yards behind them, Georgene's creamy body flashed by.

"Clay!" Sadie gasped.

The hatless Croaker pulled his horse about as he neared her, spinning around to face his attacker and lifting his gun again. Clay was turning Georgene in a wide circle to come back to them. She wanted to scream his name and tell him to go back. It was too dangerous! But there wasn't enough time for that.

She rolled the rock in her hand and pitched it at the back of the Croaker's red horse. It hit the tender thigh muscle above the joint, and the horse exploded. It screamed and leapt forward, then reared back so far it nearly toppled over. The Croaker fell from his saddle with a shout. Without so much as a look behind it, the horse took off across the field, stirring up dust and causing a commotion.

Sadie sat silently for a moment, then leaned forward to peek at the downed Croaker. The man was sprawled out against the grass, eyes closed, and no gun in sight. She took a long breath, finally letting her adrenaline slow down.

Hoofbeats rattled the rocks beneath her knees, and she turned to find Georgene trotting up next to her. Her eyes trailed up the horse's body and were stabbed by the bright sun rays. She put a hand up to shield her face. Clay's black hat encircled his face, sunbeams pouring down on either side. It was almost too dark to see his face, but she didn't need to see him to feel the wash of relief. Especially when he leaned over and put out a hand to help her up.

His hand on hers was everything right in the world. She clutched it and leapt up as he hauled her onto Georgene's back behind him. She slid into place behind his saddle, wrapping her arms around his torso and leaning into him. His strong, solid form beckoned her, and she pressed every inch of her body into the back of his.

He didn't speak a word as he turned the horse away from the mess and rode on. She held back a torrent of emotion at touching Clay again, resting her nose against his shoulder and breathing in his familiar oaky scent. Her fingers pressed into the hard muscles of his chest beneath his thin shirt.

She would return with him to the hideout. She would trade a sure, safe marriage and a chance at a community for the love and passion she had with Clay. Just touching him there on fleeing horseback made her feel more alive than she had in days.

The feeling was shattered when a bullet hit the dirt next to them. His muscles tensed under her hands. She twisted to look back over her shoulder.

The hatless Croaker was up again and on the move. He whipped Clover into a full gallop, a revolver pointed at them as he yelled into the wind.

Clay reached back to loop an arm through her knee as he urged Georgene to pick up the pace, weaving in and out of sagebrush. Sadie grabbed hold of him as another bullet flew by.

They had to get rid of the Croaker. There was no way they'd make it all the way to the trees with that guy on their tail. He was too close, and it was only a matter of time before one of his bullets found them. But Clay had his hands full. One on the reins and one on her. She debated kicking him off her leg, but the extra hold on her felt so safe and grounding. Instead, she slid a hand down his hip and pulled the revolver from his holster. With an awkward twist, she extended one arm out behind them and fired a shot.

The Croaker ducked and shouted obscenities. Clover bellowed her discomfort, and Sadie bit into her lip. She said a silent prayer as she aimed again, hoping her shots stayed over the mare's head.

A bump in the saddle made her second shot go wild. When one of the Croaker's bullets whizzed by her ear, she swallowed a knot of panic and steeled her nerves. She aimed again, holding just as tight to Clay as she was the revolver. The bullet exploded free and struck the Croaker square in the chest. He flipped off the back of the horse as if he'd been jerked from behind. With a somersault through the air, he landed in a dust cloud on the ground.

Her body collapsed against Clay's in relief.

Georgene slowed, and they turned in a tight circle to survey the attackers behind them. The tips of the grass moved in the wind, but the only other movement was that of Clover as she plodded slowly toward them.

The threat was gone.

Clay pulled the buckskin mare to a stop and threw his leg over her neck to slide. When he stood next to Sadie and reached for her waist, the rim of his hat tipped into the air, and the sunlight caught his eyes. She'd never seen them so bright and open or creased in concern.

Her heart melted into his awaiting hands.

His fingers around her waist were gentle but firm as he lifted her from the back of the horse and lowered her to the ground in front of him. Then those hands were in her hair, sliding up the back of her neck and molding his fingers into her, just as she'd imagined him doing for the last three nights.

"I saw you and your horse crash into that fella. And—and you flew off. Are you okay?"

His head lowered, covering her with the edge of his hat, and he touched his forehead to hers.

She closed her eyes, letting the very feel and smell of him envelop her, but she was reluctant to reach out for him completely yet.

"I'm alive," she whispered. "On the outside at least."

His fingers gripped tighter in her hair, and she could almost swear she heard a catch in his breath.

"What are you doing out here?" he asked.

"Running. I thought I might be able to find the hideout. I needed to talk to you."

He pulled them apart just far enough to look down at her. His eyes held her tight, and she struggled for resolve. If she didn't get out what she wanted to say, she was afraid she'd let him sweep her away and never be able to again.

"I'm all ears for you, darlin'."

Her throat itched and threatened to close up, but she swallowed her nerves and pushed through. "This has been a horrifying experience, coming to terms with what I thought was the truth and what was real. With both Papa and you." She flexed her fingers against the side of her dress, fidgeting and trying to push the words out before they escaped. "I always thought I was where I was supposed to be and doing what I was supposed to do. Then I found out it was all wrong. All a lie."

"Just because Jed Tanner was not your father does not mean he didn't love you."

"I know." Tears tickled her eyes. "Just because you're not who he chose for me does not mean you're not the best choice."

He drew in a long breath as he fit his warm palm against her cheek.

"I've never felt so lost and empty than the last few days," she continued. "Living without you. Trying to survive without seeing you. Hearing you." Her hands finally trembled up his chest and held onto the strong muscles of his neck and shoulders. "Touching you."

The moment that her eyes lowered, he tucked a finger under her chin and lifted her head up to look at him. She bit back the tears, overwhelmed by both love and fear.

"I don't want to feel that ever again," she whispered.

"I don't want you to either." His thumb caressed over her cheek. "Being without you has been torture. I didn't know I could feel such pain as when you turned me away at the barn. Somehow I thought I would be enough for you."

Regret choked her. She never should have turned him away.

"The Clay I met in the forest is. The one who kissed me next to the river and visited my cabin in the woods is. Before

Ace poked his nose into things. I love that Clay, and I want him."

He moved in closer to her, lips nearly brushing hers. She pulled in his breath, sliding her fingers back into his long honey locks. She could feel the warmth of his lips as he spoke.

"That Clay is waiting for you. He didn't make it out of town unscathed. I've never cared what the people of town—any town—thought of me for my entire life until I went there with you. Hearing the denial on your beautiful lips was agony."

"I will never deny you again."

"I'm glad to hear that, darlin'. Here's your chance."

Sadie frowned. Then she realized his face wasn't as close to hers anymore. His eyes stared over her head, and she spun around.

Emerald Falls lay several hundred yards to the south of them. Approaching in less than half that distance was a familiar black horse.

Robert Murphy.

CHAPTER 23

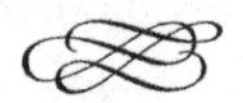

Robert's horse slid to a stop a couple wagon lengths away from them, and he drew his rifle. His brow was creased and eyes wild under a smear of red sweaty dirt.

"Run, Sadie!" he shouted as he pointed the rifle in Clay's direction.

Clay grabbed Sadie by the arm and stepped around her, drawing his revolver.

"No, stop!" Sadie slapped a hand out to block the handgun.

Clay looked at her in surprise, but she pressed a forearm into his chest to back him up a step. His eyes snapped back to Robert, but he complied, moving back at her request until she was in front of him again. She pushed his revolver back to his hip, and he lowered it, reholstering the gun with a quick spin.

"What's going on, Sadie?" Clay murmured through a tight jaw.

She fought the urge to run her fingers over the taut muscles in his face, the alluring stubble on his chin. She didn't want him to be so vexed, especially because of her. Instead, she patted an open palm lightly on his chest, letting it linger as she turned to glance at Robert over her shoulder.

"He's no threat," she said. "He probably doesn't even know how to shoot that gun."

Robert's face tightened, and his nose curled into a snarl. He readjusted the rifle on his shoulder.

"Sadie," he called, hesitation marring his voice. "Step away from that man before he hurts you."

She turned to face him, setting her hands on her hips. When she didn't budge, his eyebrows moved in a mix of confusion and annoyance.

"Hurry, step away," he said. "I've got him in my sights. He can just leave in that direction, and we will go home."

The crease in her brow grew, and she took a step backward with a defiant narrow of her eyes. When her back touched Clay's chest, she dropped a hand behind her to catch his, bringing it around her waist. Clay needed little persuasion, and he held her tight about her ribs.

Robert looked between the two of them with growing agitation. "What is this?" he barked.

"I don't need rescuing, Robert," she said with an even tone. "I may have before, but that time has passed. There's nothing I need rescuing from."

"This man," Robert spat, glaring up and down Clay's form, "he's not from around here. Do you even know him?"

Sadie tilted her head back to look up at Clay. His face was stoic, calm, shadowed by his hat, but even in the dark, his eyes glowed for her. Held her and caressed her without the slightest movement. The primal urge he conjured within her was a drive so strong she could not deny it. She stretched a hand over her shoulder and ran her fingers up along the rough underside of his jaw and trailed them down the tender flesh of his throat.

Without letting her eyes fall away from his, she spoke aloud.

"Of course I know him. I know him more than any other person in this world, and I am a better person because of it."

Clay's face remained solid, but his eyes twinkled in the corners. His fingers pressed into her ribs, pulling her even closer to his body. She was tempted to turn and press into him, to just tackle him to the ground there in the field.

Robert snorted a dirty and disgusted laugh. "Are you serious? You and this stranger? Such a filthy dove."

Clay's chin popped up, and he glared at the other man. Robert flinched slightly, dropping a hand on his rifle to his reins.

A grin twitched on her lips at Robert's reaction. His words stung, but they held so little weight to her anymore.

Perhaps it'd been silly to allow a stranger to soil her when she'd had an agreeable man ready to marry her. But she thanked her stars for it. To find out how truly boring and ungentlemanly Robert was before she'd married him was a blessing. To find a man so beautiful and passionate as Clay, someone that lifted up her soul and made her feel alive, was an even bigger one.

Nothing Robert said to her could destroy her anymore.

Clay's muscles were tense against her. Like a loaded spring. She pressed back against him in hopes of calming him. Then she glared at Robert.

"Go on home," she said. "I'm sure there are plenty of woman back there who will have you."

"Of course there are," he said. "They'll be better fits for me too. At least my wife won't be raising my daughters to wear pants and shoot guns."

"Well someone in the relationship has to," Clay snorted.

Robert snarled, turning his fidgeting horse in a circle. "I

should have known you were too different. No amount of money is worth fostering a sloppily-dressed whore."

Sadie gasped, but she had little time to be offended. She stumbled to the side as Clay pushed his way through her. His revolver was in the air, and she cried out as she reached for him.

He was too fast.

A shot pinged off metal. Robert yelped, throwing his reverberating rifle to the ground. Then another shot. A cloud of dust exploded from his hat as the bullet struck it, and his horse jumped up with a squeal, nearly knocking him to the ground. With a horror-stricken look back, Robert rammed his heels into his horse, and the two took off over the wide-open field, headed back to Emerald Falls.

Sadie leapt into Clay's arms and folded into him. He holstered his gun and embraced her fully, curling around her shoulder to press his nose into her neck. His warm breath on her ear sent chills down her spine.

"He's a fool," he breathed. "I hope one day you'll teach our children to be just as spunky and strong as you."

She pulled back to look at him, but his hands were already on her face, in her hair, claiming her even as his lips found hers. He tasted like heaven, a familiar sensation she'd been longing for. Electricity sparked through her, and she hopped into his arms as he lifted her from the ground.

"I thought I'd never kiss you again," he groaned between feverish kisses.

She wrapped her legs around his hips and choked back a threatening spring of tears as she ran her fingernails down his back. "I couldn't live with the thought of it," she whispered.

"You'll never have to again."

~

Clay stopped Georgene on the edge of the trees, and Sadie could feel the tension grow heavy in his muscles. The afternoon sun cast the group of tents and horses grazing along the perimeter of the clearing in a warm orange glow. A familiar soft rumble of voices and the casual ambiance of camp life reached them, and Sadie's heart swelled. She'd never imagined she'd miss it when she'd first been brought to the camp. That she'd ever turn her life upside down to run back to it.

She lifted her cheek from Clay's shoulder and sat back as he dismounted. He was just sliding her down to join him when someone among the tents shouted.

They turned as one to find Clara marching toward them with a beaming smile and open arms.

"Sadie Tanner, as I live and breathe. I never thought I'd see your face again."

Sadie grinned, overwhelmed by the rush upon seeing Clara. She hurried past Clay and into the other woman's arms, hugging her right back.

"I was afraid you wouldn't," she panted into Clara's shoulder.

The blonde held her at arm's length with a toothy grin. "I knew you two were inseparable forces. It was only a matter of time until you crashed together." Clara's nose wrinkled as she winked.

A blush crept into Sadie's cheeks. "I'm glad you had faith in it. It was a frightening ordeal at times."

Clara waved the thought away. "Of course. Love is a risk. You wouldn't be normal if you weren't a little afraid."

Sadie wanted to mention that she hadn't heard of love typically including shootouts, but Clay stepped up behind her and stole her thoughts away.

"Look what the beautiful lady dragged in," Clara scoffed,

popping her hip out. “I was starting to think we weren’t going to see you again either.”

Sadie frowned, glancing over her shoulder at Clay. He gave a stiff nod.

“Thanks for the welcome.”

“Oh, I’m happy to see you for sure, but I may be the only one. Come on.”

Clara led the way into the tent clusters, and Sadie’s hand found Clay’s. He held tight to her fingers as she leaned into his arm to whisper.

“What happened, Clay?”

“I haven’t been back to camp since I lost you. They probably think I’m dead.”

Her insides clenched, and she tugged on his arm, bringing him to a stop in the shade of a stray tree.

“That was days ago,” she hissed. “Where have you been?”

He regarded her with a quiet reserve. "Emerald Falls. Here and there. Keeping watch over the Murphy plantation."

“Are you crazy? Aren’t you supposed to lay low after you rob someone?”

“Sure. But what if someone robs me? Am I supposed to just go home and forget about it?”

Her voice disappeared, gone with her breath. She pulled harder on his arm and snagged the back of his neck, pressing a possessive kiss to his lips. His words settled deep within her bones, but she had no reply to his confession.

He’d waited for her. Watched out for her. Risked his life to remain near her.

She wished she’d been so loyal.

She was happy to spend the rest of her life making it up to him.

Clay’s lips hummed softly into her kiss, and he rested his forehead against hers.

Clara cleared her throat, and Clay looked up. A crowd

was heading toward them. Ace led the way, followed by a scowling Tom and a few other men. Ginny and Bridget hurried along behind them.

"Clay Pearson," Ace boomed, arms open wide but one of his brows tilted in question. "I was starting to think someone had picked you up. Thank goodness you made it home, and with a visitor I see."

"What the hell are you doing?" Tom barked, pushing his way up alongside Ace and glaring at his brother.

"I'm coming home after a few days on the prairie," Clay said with an annoyed edge in his voice. "I thought you'd be happy to see me."

"Happy? You didn't follow through on getting this girl to St. Aspen on time. Probably blew our deal wide open. What the hell were you thinking?"

"I was thinking I didn't give a shit about the deal. She's not for sale. It was a bad deal anyway."

Tom's face contorted with rage, and he puffed up, stepping up to Clay. "You think my idea was shit? We could have gotten a lot of money for her if you hadn't ruined it. You were on board in the beginning! What the hell happened?"

Sadie felt so small next to the yelling men, and Clay's hand was crushing hers. When he bowed up against Tom, she let go and took a step back.

"You want to know what happened? When you heard that man's name on the train, you spun off into one of your brilliant ideas. That's fine. I like to contribute to Ace's cause as much as the next guy, but your scheme quickly went from kidnapping that man to taking him and his innocent daughter. Then you got him killed!"

The tendons in Clay's neck were standing out, and she fought the urge to reach out and smooth her fingers over them to calm him. But he was in no state for soothing.

"I didn't," Tom spat. "The idiot got shot. And not by me."

"It was your idea," Clay growled. "Your responsibility. The deal went sour. It was a flop. We can pick up a new one."

"The hell with that," Tom snarled. "I'll take her in myself." He reached a hand over to snag Sadie's sleeve.

Clay's body snapped. Sadie gasped as he leapt forward, and Tom's fingers were snatched away from her. Clay slammed his brother back against the tree next to them, pinning him by his throat.

Tom's wide eyes blinked and rolled as he collected his bearings. When Clay's fingers squeezed around his neck, they snapped to him.

"You will not lay a finger on her," Clay breathed. "She's not a part of your plan any longer. She's mine."

A primal satisfaction writhed within Sadie's chest, and she couldn't help but reach out to Clay's free hand. It rested just behind his revolver, and she wound her fingers with his. His body eased at her touch, and he turned to look back at her.

"Come on, Clay. He's your brother," she murmured.

Dirty pig of a man or not, Tom was the last family Clay had left. She ran her fingers over his knuckles and coaxed him away. Clay turned to glare back at his brother and released him. Tom cleared his throat, straightening his shirt without looking up at either of them. Then he turned and strode away.

The group stood in silence a moment before Ace stepped forward.

"I'm just glad to see you back in one piece, my friend." He clapped Clay on the shoulder, draining most of the tension from his body.

"I'm sorry I ruined the plan."

Ace nodded with tight lips. As he began to speak, Sadie stepped forward.

"It wouldn't have mattered," she said. "My aunt would never have paid you."

Ace frowned with a perked eyebrow.

"She did write you back. I found the letter while we were in town. It's...well, it's gone now, but Clay read it too."

Clay nodded. "I did. She said she refused to send any money."

Ace let out a long breath as he rubbed at the dark hair on his chin. "Then it sounds like everything ended as it should have. We weren't going to get paid, and Miss Tanner here needed a new family."

The smile on Ace's face was more genuinely friendly and welcoming than she'd ever seen it. It moved her to a place of even greater peace, and she smiled back.

"Welcome to our camp, my dear," he said, taking her hand. "Again."

"Thank you," she said.

Clay cleared his throat, narrowing his eyes and giving Ace a jaunt of his chin. Ace let go of Sadie with a grin and hands in the air.

"Of course. Well, I'm sure you both have plenty of stories for us. Shall we gather around the campfire for dinner?"

Clay smiled. "Wouldn't miss it. We'll be right there."

Ace gave a two-finger salute, and the gang meandered back into the center of camp.

Clay pulled Sadie in close, and she slipped into his arms, feeling on top of the world and the most grounded she'd ever been. He leaned in close, sliding the brim of his hat along the top of her head and shrouding them both in the shadow of the afternoon sun.

"Bet you're glad I waited around the plantation like an idiot now, hmm?" he breathed.

She chuckled, rubbing her nose along his. His lips captured hers and stole her breath away.

"Thank you for believing in me," she whispered across his lips, "you stubborn ass."

His chuckle was deep and warm. "I love you, Sadie Tanner."

Her body ignited in excitement and an influx of emotion. She trailed her fingers down his cheek as she kissed him again. "I love you too."

He lifted her off the ground and spun a lazy circle with her cradled against his chest, a warm smile on his face. "You'll never be without a family or love again."

EPILOGUE

Sadie stood alongside Clay in the cool morning air, pressed in against his ribs and nestled under his arm. On his other side, he propped an elbow on a long-handled shovel and admired his handy work.

"It looks perfect, Clay. Thank you," she said.

The yellow daffodils she'd picked on the way that morning swayed in the breeze up against the wooden cross Clay had erected there beneath a wide, old aspen tree. She'd helped him build the cross the day before and carve the large letters into the grain.

Jed Tanner it read in neat scroll, just below the etching of a single sprawl of an elk antler Clay had carved with a railroad tine. Sadie hadn't known he could create such beautiful things, and she'd leaned over him the entire hour it'd taken him to produce the perfect marker for her father's grave.

Or at least, Jed Tanner's grave.

She wasn't sure she'd ever be able to come to terms with the truth about Papa. He'd loved her, and she'd loved him, and no proof in letters would change that.

No amounts of troubled past would change her direction

now. After three days of living in the Van den Berg camp as a new member rather than a prisoner, she felt like part of the family. Three days of living in Clay's tent had been even better.

He'd taught her so many ways to love a body and a soul. She was drunk on learning him.

More than that, she was thankful. She'd found her place in the world and gained a community after all, and she couldn't be happier.

"Thank you for all of this," she whispered, rubbing her nose into the hollow of his shoulder. "Taking care of my father."

"Of course," he said, voice deep and raspy in her hair.

"And for taking care of me." She found his eyes. The deep blue ones that still sent electricity through her like a chill. "I never knew my life could be so happy and fulfilled until I met you."

He rested a palm against her cheek, running his thumb over her nose and lip. "I should thank you for the same. My life before you was answering to Tom and Ace. I didn't question it. I had nothing worth fighting for."

She smiled, and he leaned forward to kiss her. She melted against him.

When his lips broke from hers, she could feel his smile, then his breath. "Let's go home."

Thank you for reading!

I hope you enjoyed Sadie and Clay's adventure in finding love in the Wild West! I love getting lost on the wild frontier, following the cowboys and outlaws as they attempt to navigate the right side of the law. Above all else, we all need a little love! And you know who else in Emerald Falls deserves a little genuine affection? Why the local reformed prostitute of the Van den Berg gang, Ginny, of course.

If you enjoyed the beginning of the Emerald Falls series, please consider leaving a review. Word of mouth is a book's best friend! Even a single small sentence helps spread its love around.

To stay on top of new releases and exclusive content, sign up for my emails at https://ivymcadams.com/subscribe

To catch up with Ginny, check out Seduced by a Wrangler or read ahead for a preview of her story!

The Emerald Falls series continues with Seduced by a Wrangler.

Turn the page to read a sample now!

Ginny meets Noah…

The saloon itself was in good shape, faded paint on the walls, sturdy columns in the middle of the wide room to accommodate the second floor above, and large paintings hanging along any wall not containing a window. A piano with an energetic older man bouncing on the keys stood against the wall opposite the bar and a few tables with chairs dotted the floor. The one closest to the front window had drawn a crowd around what sounded like a game of poker.

Men lingered here and there around the room, some speaking and laughing with one another, some hovering next to ladies dressed in lacy dresses that pushed their bosoms up and out and showed far too much leg.

Things Ginny used to wear, including those fake smiles and batting eyelashes.

Thank goodness those days were behind her.

She'd take the thin lavender dress she wore, nearly day in and day out, over all that mess any day.

Those fancy clothes came at a high price.

As she made her way further into the saloon, a cloud of smoke hit her and she coughed into her elbow. Her eyes burned, and she struggled to get past a pair of smokers and over to the bar.

The smell of tobacco and sweat was strong, and she pressed the back of her wrist beneath her nose. Just as she reached the bar, however, something else hit her. Something much more pleasant. She dropped her arm and drew in a deep breath, casting her eyes side to side. She started when the man she'd just past looked up from his drink.

His faded brown wide-brimmed hat lifted, and his light eyes met hers.

For a moment her breath was gone. His soft blue eyes were shadowed by his hat, but she didn't miss them twitch left and right, as if unsure where to settle. His jaw was firm, smooth but for a whisper of dark hair on his chin, and his lips looked soft and inviting. He had to be one of the best looking cowboys she'd run into in a bar.

The thought sent a roll of butterflies through her stomach.

But why was he looking at her like that?

Had he heard her sniff him?

An itchy warmth spread into her cheeks, and she chuckled aloud to herself as she perched against the bar a few feet away from him. She didn't make a habit of smelling men, but she thought about walking by him twice.

She tilted her chin in his direction.

"Hey."

His eyes moved again, creasing a little at the edges when they settled on her, then he tilted his chin up. "Hey."

His voice was deep and rolled like a well-oiled wagon wheel.

She smiled at him. "What you drinking?"

He peered down at the clearly labeled bottle of beer in his hand. "Carters Beer."

One of her eyebrows perked as she leaned further into the bar. "Sounds good. Hey, I'll have one of those." Her voice lifted as she snagged the bartender.

A man in faded overalls glanced between her and the cowboy and turned to fetch the drink.

"Here," a woman called as she carried in a wide crate. She was tiny, her long black hair flowing well past her waist, but set the wooden box of beers down without so much of a grunt. "We're out up here."

The bartender pulled a bottle free, popped the lid, and slid it across the bar to Ginny.

She caught it in her open palm and lifted it toward the cowboy in a toast-like manner. "A fresh one. Perfect."

His eyebrows went up a fraction, but he offered no other friendly signs.

What a stick in the mud, she thought as she lifted the beer to her lips. It wasn't as smooth as she'd hoped, but it was way better than whiskey.

When she lowered the bottle to the bartop again, she tried to keep her eyes on the stacks of bottles behind the bartender. Mostly whiskeys, a few bourbons and gins. A bowl of apples and almonds.

Over her shoulder men milled about the saloon. Three in a nearby corner guffawed so loud her insides clenched. Her eyes lingered on them, curious as to what had caused the outburst, but they returned to a normal level of speaking that she couldn't catch.

Nothing caught her eye like the cowboy at the bar. He was beautiful.

And she'd seen her fair share of men.

Even if he didn't seem up for conversation at the moment, she couldn't help herself. Her eyes and her energy were drawn to him. Another few words wouldn't hurt.

She leaned toward him again, a growing smile on her face. "You from around here, or you just—"

Two boisterous men in wide hats pushed their way up to the bar, nearly knocking her to the side and cutting off her communication to the cowboy. She stared with wide-eyes, unsure whether to be relieved that she hadn't been trampled or irked that they'd ruined her one-sided conversation.

She tilted her head, peering through the loud strangers to find that the cowboy's head was lifted again, and he was looking at her. Nerves fluttered in her stomach, and she grinned.

While the bartender brought the strangers their drinks, she sipped on hers. When they stepped away, she slid down the length of the bar to stand next to the cowboy. Before she could finish her question, he spoke.

"I'm just passing through."

She nodded, a small pang of disappointment settling in her chest, though why she had no idea. He was just some stranger in a saloon. What did she care if he was merely passing through?

She smiled just the same. "Good place to stop in for a drink."

The tip of his hat jerked as he nodded. "Yeah. Nice town. You live here?"

She shook her head, letting the mischievous tickle within her seep into her eyes. "I'm just passing through."

He cracked a grin, and her heart fluttered.

The rim of his bottle connected with his lips, and he tilted his head back to let the rest of his beer roll down his throat. She couldn't help but stare at the strong muscles in his neck as he did so. She continued to gaze at him as she took another long pull of her beer.

When his eyes met hers again, they were a little more clouded but certainly had a twinkle in them.

Ginny's body warmed beneath the surface. A spark of excitement flashed in her stomach, something she certainly was not accustomed to. Her fingers tingled, and the toe of her boot tapped along with the piano tune.

"There is one thing I do like about Emerald Falls though," she said.

He perked an eyebrow, the edge of his mouth twitching upward.

"They have some damn good music." She set her beer down and pushed off the bar. He blinked in surprise as she sidled up closer to him and offered him a hand. "Dance with me, cowboy."

He hesitated, glancing out to the open space in the middle

of the floor where only one other couple was spinning around. His lips pressed together, a small shake in his head.

"I don't really—"

She grabbed his hand resting on the bar and gave him a tug.

"Oh, come on. It's fun!"

Despite the unsure look on his face, the cowboy allowed her to pull him out onto the dance floor.

She was surprised to find that he was much taller than her when he wasn't slumped against the bar, maybe an entire foot, and she had to lean her head back to see him. She fit her hand into his and gave his shoulder a squeeze as they lined up.

His free hand hovered near her body as he gave her a look over, his lips pursed and eyes searching.

She gave a hearty laugh as she snagged his fingers and pressed them to her waist.

"I won't bite you or nothin'. Can't you dance?"

His eyes darkened as he cleared his throat. "It's been a long time."

Despite the edge in his gaze, his smoldering look set her breath tripping, and she couldn't help the intrigued bounce in her eyebrows.

"Well, here's a refresher for you," she said, pressing his hand in tighter to her waist before her grip slid back up to his shoulder.

Then she set them off, moving to the music.

The piano notes bounced, and they stepped lively along with them. The cowboy's body was stiff under her hands, but he could keep up. She grinned at him, his eyes down on their feet more than they were on her.

Her mother had taught her to dance as a girl, but it wasn't something she practiced often. Dancing wasn't typically what men came to the brothel for.

During a dip in the music, Ginny slid out from under his hand on her waist and twirled beneath his arm. She bumped his chest when she faced him again and giggled as she readjusted them.

He blinked those cool blue eyes at her, a smile tugging at the edge of his mouth.

She leaned in closer and spoke over the drumming piano keys behind them. "I'm Ginny, by the way."

He leaned in too, the edge of his cowboy hat covering her head and that tantalizing smell she'd passed earlier was trapped in her space. She took a deep, appreciative breath.

"Noah."

As the beat of the song picked up a notch, she moved faster.

Or at least she tried to. She could unlatch for a twirl and come back or even add an extra little wiggle of her hips as they moved, but Noah didn't seem to be into adding any flourish to his steps. As a matter of fact, he was still rather stiff in the arms, and she wondered if she even saw his lips move as he counted the steps beneath them.

As the music came to an end, she hung against his shoulder with a chuckle. "You need to have another beer before the next one. Loosen up."

The corner of his lip disappeared in his teeth with a solemn nod. "That would probably help, but I'm done for the night. I gotta be up early in the morning."

The excitement of the evening dropped out of her sails with an uncomfortable rush. She detached herself from him as nonchalantly as she could manage, smoothing her hands down her dress and rubbing her thumb along her jaw.

She'd just thrown herself at that guy, and to what end? She wasn't sure what she wanted. She didn't usually go looking for men. She never had to.

But she'd also never wanted to.

Disappointment stung in her chest, and she nodded.

"Sure. Of course. Got to beat the sun out of here, huh?"

He tilted his head with a slow smile, and already she was hooked again, leaning in closer to hear what he had to say.

"I've got to help make a delivery in the morning. I don't make my run, I don't get paid. I don't get paid, and I can't afford any more beer."

There was a teasing spark in his eye, and it lit her up more than she cared to admit. She grinned and giggled under her breath.

"Guess that makes sense. Nothing on the house around here."

"Never." Then his fingers brushed her elbow as he took a step back. "Nice to meet you, Ginny."

Then he was gone, walking toward the front of the saloon, and she stood on the dance floor watching his back disappear into a throng of people. His shoulders were wide and tapered down in a slim waist and a firm bottom beneath a tight pair of trousers.

She narrowed her eyes as she drank it in, producing a rumble of appreciation in her chest. A man that could wear pants like that spent his day on horseback.

She wished she could be up in the saddle with him.

ACKNOWLEDGMENTS

I dabble in writing many different genres, but I truly love romance. I love the hope I find in them. No matter what stressful things happen in the middle of the story, I know magic will happen by the end.

My biggest thanks goes to my best friend Simone. You've kept me working hard and are the best soundboard for all my plotting ideas. We've turned our writing adventure into a well-oiled machine, and I couldn't have done it without you! I'm so stoked for our adventure into the writing world together. You rock! Plus, you showed up right when I needed you the most. How'd you do that? No matter. I'm so glad you did!

Also a big thanks to my mother, even if I'm going to pretend she doesn't read my steamy books. She kept a huge bookcase of romance novels in our house when I was growing up. I'm sure she turned an equally blind eye that I was sneaking off with them as a teen and devouring them.

ALSO BY IVY MCADAMS

Emerald Falls Series

Kidnapped by an Outlaw

Seduced by a Wrangler

Captivated by a Gunslinger

Emerald Falls Novella

Rescued by a Desperado

ABOUT THE AUTHOR

Ivy McAdams wants to be a cowgirl when she grows up.

She may reside on the beaches of Florida, but her heart lives in the wide open spaces of Wyoming. She grew up dreaming of horses, playing cowboys and indians on her grandfather's farm, and curling up on the couch with him to watch westerns. Cowboys have been her heroes ever since.

Ivy loves the warm feelings and happily ever afters of a romance novel and has married her passions together to bring you historical western romance stories.

When not writing, she's taking care of two beautiful girls and teaching them to adore books as much as she did growing up. She can't wait until they're big enough to dress in cowboy hats and ride horses with her.

https://ivymcadams.com

facebook.com/ivymcadams

instagram.com/authorivymcadams

twitter.com/ivylovesbooks

goodreads.com/ivymcadams

bookbub.com/profile/ivy-mcadams

Made in the USA
Monee, IL
09 June 2021

70769948R00142